THE OVERLOOKED SENTIENCE

ABHISHEK UDAY SALVI

INDIA • SINGAPORE • MALAYSIA

ISBN

Hardcase 979-8-89415-612-5
Paperback 979-8-89415-019-2

Disclaimer:

Contents

Contents

Contents

Story 4
Gentle Giants

Introduction

The book explores the idea that the wide spectrum of emotions such as Joy, Fear, Pain, and Love are not unique to humans but rather shared across different living organisms. The author aims to capture readers' attention and focus on four fictional narratives involving various intelligent species. These stories aim to demonstrate that animals have a wide range of emotions similar to those experienced by humans.

The book reflects on a troubling aspect of human behavior: our tendency to ignore or downplay the deep emotional connections between different species. This disregard stems from our self-centered desires and pursuits. The book emphasizes that because we prioritize our own wants and needs, we often overlook the complex emotional bonds that form between these magnificent creatures. As a result, these creatures are denied the experience of profound emotions they are inherently capable of.

The author highlights the urgent need to address the destructive consequences of human greed and selfishness through four fictional stories. It acknowledges that our relentless desires have led to the endangerment and extinction of numerous species. As a powerful call to action, the book asserts that the present moment is a turning point and urges an immediate cessation of exploitative practices.

The book's final plea is compelling: it's high time to revolutionize our approach toward these sentient beings. It advocates for granting these creatures the lives they inherently deserve, free from human exploitation and informed by a recognition of their capacity for emotions and experiences that mirror our own. By raising our awareness and transforming our actions, we can bridge the gap we have created and pave the way for a more harmonious coexistence for all living beings.

Story 1

Queen's Last Stand

Chapter 1

A Legacy of Hunting

The Ranthambore Wildlife Sanctuary, once envisioned as a sanctuary of safety, emerged as a battleground between humanity's greed and the indomitable spirit of the wild. This tale poignantly reminds us that no sanctuary or haven is truly impenetrable in the face of human desires.

In the archives of time, tales of grand hunting expeditions embellished with opulence and extravagance painted a vivid picture of a bygone era. The mighty Maharajas, seeking to demonstrate their prowess and dominance, set their sights on the most formidable prey—the regal tiger. These majestic beings, rulers of the jungle, were hunted relentlessly, their lives reduced to mere trophies, symbols of the rulers' might and valor. Tigers became targets of conquest, paraded in victory, and used to showcase the power of the rulers who had captured them. It was a dark age when the hunting of these magnificent creatures had become an emblem of prestige and supremacy.

As the legacy of hunting extended its claws through time, the chapter journeyed forward to witness the shifting motives behind these relentless pursuits. The opulence and grandeur of the past had eventually given way to a darker and more sinister practice—Poaching. In the modern era, driven by greed and demand for tiger skins, bones, and teeth in the name of traditional medicine, poachers roamed the wilderness with ruthless intent. The lust for wealth and the promise of exorbitant prices in the black market had transformed the once-respected tiger into a mere commodity, a means to a profit-driven end.

This evolution of the legacy of hunting, born out of human greed, spoke of a troubling and tragic transformation. What was once an act of valor and pride had devolved into want for destruction. The once-venerated tiger, guardian of the jungle and emblem of power, had become a victim of human exploitation.

In the heart of this perilous environment, amidst the dense foliage of the Ranthambore Wildlife Sanctuary, we introduce our central character—Rani, the tigress. The forest officials bestowed her name, meaning "Queen", as she represented a sense of royalty and strength, a fitting tribute to her wild and untamed spirit. Rani was a living embodiment of her kind's regal and dignified nature, a guardian of the forest, and a symbol of the enduring spirit of the wild. She's a healthy 4-year-old tigress weighing almost 170 kg, with a length of about 8 ft and a height of about 3.5 ft.

Rani's world was not isolated; three innocent and vulnerable cubs depended on her to survive. This was her first litter. The cubs were four months old, two males and one female. There was a tender and fierce bond between the mother and her cubs, a testament to the unyielding love and dedication of maternal instinct. Despite the looming threat of human exploitation, Rani fiercely protected and nurtured her young.

The air was thick with the scent of history as the tale of Rani, the tigress, began to unfold in the majestic wilderness of the Ranthambore Wildlife Sanctuary. This chapter embarks on a journey through time, delving into the dark and haunting legacy of tiger hunting, a practice that had etched its mark upon the landscape and the very soul of these enigmatic creatures. Once revered as symbols of power and royalty, Tigers had fallen prey to the insatiable appetite for sport and conquest among the Maharajas and Britishers.

Chapter 2

The Struggle to Survive

As the scorching summer sun beats down on Rajasthan's arid landscape, life becomes increasingly challenging for the inhabitants of the Ranthambore Wildlife Sanctuary. The sweltering heat intensifies the struggle for survival, and for Rani, the tigress, it means the daunting task of providing for her four-month-old cubs.

For the next two years, the young cubs depend entirely on Rani's care and protection. They are still learning the ways of the wild, and every day brings new lessons in the art of survival. Their soft, furry coats and wide, curious eyes are a stark reminder of the vulnerability of life in the wild.

Rani, known for her exceptional hunting skills and majestic presence, has become a significant tourist attraction in the Sanctuary. She was the daughter of the famous tigress named Machli. Machli had died a few years back, and Rani was the new owner of Machli's territory. Rani had learned hunting skills from her veteran mother. Visitors worldwide come to glimpse this regal tigress in her natural habitat. But amidst the admiration and fascination of the tourists lies the reality of the harsh and unforgiving wilderness. Forest Rangers had planned to put a GPS collar on her neck. Unfortunately, there was a procurement delay for the new enhanced GPS devices.

Hunting becomes a daunting challenge as the days grow hotter, even for a skilled predator like Rani. The searing temperatures drive most prey species into the safety of shade and water sources during the scorching hours of the day. The lack of available prey means Rani must venture further deep into the jungle and search harder for her meal. At the same time, she wants to avoid entering another tiger's territory.

The struggle to find food is compounded by the responsibility of caring for her cubs. Rani's maternal instincts drove her to prioritize the well-being of her offspring above her own needs. This means feeding her milk to them on an empty stomach. The best way now was scavenging. At times, she had to rely on the hunt of a more successful carnivore and tiger's rival – a Leopard. They are no match for tigers, yet they have a higher hunting success rate than tigers because of their stealth tactics. On numerous occasions, she remained on the scraps left behind by the Leopard.

The continuous search for food took a toll on Rani's strength and endurance. As the days passed, she lost weight and became leaner. Tigers must feed once or twice weekly to maintain their muscular frame. A tiger can eat around 35 kg of meat at once.

As the sun sets on the horizon, the day's heat begins to wane, and the coolness of the evening breathes a momentary respite. This is when Rani becomes more active, utilizing her stealth and hunting prowess to its full potential. The cover of darkness gives her the advantage she needs to move silently through the dense foliage, and night hunting is less taxing on her body. Furthermore, there is no disturbance from the annoying baboons, monkeys, or birds who always alert the entire region of her presence.

The silence of the night is broken by the call of nocturnal creatures and the rustle of leaves as Rani stalks her prey. Her keen senses come into play, and she becomes one with the shadows, a ghostly presence in the moonlit landscape. The moon casts an ethereal glow on her orange and black stripes, transforming her into a creature of mythical beauty.

In this moment of tranquility, Rani seizes her chance. She spots a herd of deer grazing in the open field, unaware of her presence. Among them is a tired deer trying to get a brief rest. Rani knows it will be an easier target, a meal that will replenish her energy and nourish her cubs.

With the precision of a seasoned hunter, she stealthily approaches her target, her powerful muscles coiled and ready to pounce. The tall grass hides her presence from the watchful eyes of the herd, and the wind carries away any hint of her scent. She gets closer and closer, her eyes locked on the unsuspecting deer.

But just as she prepares to launch her surprise attack, a rustling noise nearby alerts the herd to potential danger. The deer scatters in a flurry of hooves, and Rani is left crouching in the shadows, her opportunity lost. Her stomach growls in frustration, but she knows that patience and persistence are her greatest allies in this unforgiving landscape. Rani tried several times, but the deer were already on high alert.

Rani's determination remains unyielding as the nights pass and the days blend into each other. Her instincts guide her, and she adapts her strategies to the changing conditions of the Sanctuary. Despite the challenges and the hardships, she is a symbol of resilience and strength, a true queen of the wild.

Rani sets out on another hunting expedition the following day, ensuring her cubs remain safely concealed in the den. This time, she decides to explore the area around a small pond within her territory. The pond is uniquely positioned, with only one entry and exit point, surrounded on three sides by small hills. This geographical advantage offers her an excellent vantage point to observe potential prey. The small pond becomes a lifeline for the animals in the territory, drawing them in for a drink and a moment of respite. The hills surrounding the pond create a natural enclosure, making it a perfect spot for the tigress to observe and strategize her hunt.

As she climbs onto a ridge overlooking the pond, she patiently spends hours scanning the surroundings. The sun reaches its highest point in the sky, marking the day's peak. A group of deer approaches the pond, unaware of the lurking danger. With keen timing, the tigress waits for the deer to relax and confidently enter the water. She knows the perfect moment to strike.

Suddenly, she leaps from her elevated position, hurtling swiftly toward the pond. She sprints toward the herd with remarkable agility, targeting a young fawn. The forest erupts in alarm—birds screech and monkeys chatter warnings. The deer scatter in different directions, but the disoriented fawn leaps further into the lake. Unlike deer, tigers are excellent swimmers. Within seconds, she catches the young fawn, her powerful jaws gripping its throat firmly.

The tigress swims back to shore with her prize, dragging it onto dry land. The fawn struggles, but her grip is solid and unyielding. Due to lack of oxygen, the young fawn succumbs in moments. She begins feasting right away, getting fueled by the taste of victory.

Nature can be brutal; one creature's death ensures another's survival. Though a modest meal enough to sustain her for a day or two, this successful hunt showcases the tigress's hunting prowess and resourcefulness in providing for herself and her cubs.

Chapter 3

Unwelcomed Neighbor

Tigers, majestic creatures of the wild, exhibit strong territorial instincts as part of their nature. These magnificent felines mark their territories with a distinctive scent—their urine. It is a proclamation to all other tigers: "Stay away; this territory is mine." Tigers rarely cross into the territories of others except for the purpose of mating. This instinct is deeply ingrained in their behavior, an essential aspect of their survival strategy.

In the intricate web of tiger relationships, a similar tale unfolded between Rani and her neighbor, Shashi. Shashi, the father of Rani's litter, shared a complex relationship with her. Tigers, by nature, are not social animals. The connection between Rani and Shashi was solely confined to the act of mating, and beyond that, they led solitary lives within their defined territories.

Shashi, the larger, stronger, and more aggressive of the two, occasionally encroached into Rani's territory for hunting purposes. Shashi had a GPS collar around its neck. While tigers are not typically sociable, their territorial boundaries are fiercely defended. Shashi used his physical superiority in this dynamic to venture into Rani's domain. Despite Rani's disapproval, a direct confrontation with Shashi in a full-fledged face-off would inevitably defeat her. Therefore, she reluctantly allowed his intrusions, knowing that resisting would only lead to a losing battle.

The consequence of Shashi's incursions into Rani's territory was reduced prey availability for her. In the relentless pursuit of survival, Rani was caught in the delicate balance between protecting her offspring and safeguarding her territory. It became an everyday struggle for the tigress—a relentless battle for sustenance, raising her litter, and maintaining the integrity of her domain.

To comprehend the intricacies of this daily survival challenge, one must delve into the life of a tigress, navigating the complexities of motherhood and territorial defense. The vast wild expanse becomes both a playground and a battlefield for these creatures. Each day, Rani faces the daunting task of providing for her cubs while simultaneously fending off the challenges of Shashi's imposing presence.

In the wild, survival is not guaranteed; it is earned through wit, strength, and adaptability. Rani's journey reflects the resilience of tigresses facing these harsh realities in her own environment. The ebb and flow of life in the wild demands constant negotiation between nurturing the next generation and securing one's place in the natural order.

As Rani traverses the landscape, the significance of her territorial markings becomes evident. The scent of her urine serves as both a warning to potential intruders and a declaration of ownership. Tigers' territory is synonymous with life, and Rani guards hers with unwavering determination.

However, on numerous occasions, Rani has faced challenges as Shashi occasionally encroached in to her territory and seized her successful kills. In these situations, Rani found herself compelled to wait until Shashi's hunger was satiated before she could partake in the bounty of her own hunting efforts.

On one such evening, as the sun dipped below the horizon, Shashi appeared on the fringes of Rani's territory. She had just brought down a Sambar and was about to enjoy her meal when Shashi's imposing figure emerged from the shadows.

"You're here again, Shashi," Rani growled, her frustration evident. "Must you always take what isn't yours?"

Shashi strolled closer; his eyes fixed on the fresh kill. "You know how it is, Rani. Survival of the fittest. If you can't defend your prey, it becomes mine."

Rani sighed, knowing that a direct confrontation would only lead to her defeat. "One day, Shashi, this arrangement will cost us both."

Shashi, now tearing into the Sambar, glanced up with a smirk. "Until then, Rani, you'll have to learn to live with it."

Despite her reservations, allowing Shashi into her territory was a calculated compromise—a testament to the instinctive understanding that a direct confrontation would be futile. Soon, Rani learned a more innovative way to deal with Shashi. She altered her strategy whenever she sensed his presence nearby during her hunts.

The next time Rani spotted Shashi from a distance, she decided to target domestic goats, which are easier to kill than wild prey. Ignoring the inevitable human confrontation that comes with hunting domestic animals, she brought down two goats. As expected, Shashi promptly appeared.

"Feast for me, I see," he said, his voice dripping with arrogance.

Rani didn't respond. Instead, she swiftly moved on to the next killed goat. By the time Shashi finished his meal, he looked up to find Rani already done feasting on another goat. "Clever," he muttered, a hint of grudging respect in his tone.

Rani glanced at him briefly, her eyes filled with quiet determination. "I have to be, Shashi. Unlike you, I have more mouths to feed." Recognizing the truth in her words, Shashi remained silent.

Rani continued to hunt with this strategy, ensuring she could enjoy her meal even in his unwelcome presence. This new approach became a testament to Rani's resilience and adaptability in the face of relentless challenges.

Chapter 4

Hunting Lessons

The cubs were now old enough to start learning the art of survival from Rani. She gathered them close and established some essential ground rules. "Alright, my little ones, come together. It's time for an important lesson," she called out, her eyes gleaming with wisdom and care.

One of the cubs piped up curiously, "What's the lesson today, Mom?"

"Today, my darlings," Rani began, "I will teach you the art of staying hidden when I'm away hunting. Listen carefully; this knowledge is crucial for your survival."

"Why do we need to stay hidden, Mom?" another cub asked, tilting its head in confusion.

Rani's expression grew serious. "There are many dangers in the Sanctuary, my sweet cub. Besides having to watch out for other predators like leopards, wild dogs—also known as dholes—and even male tigers, there's a bigger threat: Humans."

The third cub's eyes widened. "Humans? But why, Mom?"

"Humans can be unpredictable and, at times, dangerous. They might try to capture or harm us, so staying out of their sight is essential. Remember to find a good hiding spot and stay quiet."

"Where do we hide, Mom?" asked one of the cubs, eager to learn.

"Hide deep in our den and never venture out without me. If you do, use the shadows, my love. The dense foliage, tall grasses, and rocks can be your allies. Blend in with your surroundings, and don't make unnecessary noises."

One cub couldn't contain its curiosity. "But what if we want to follow you, Mom? We want to learn how to hunt!"

Rani's stern gaze softened with a smile. "Ah, that's the next lesson. Next time, I will take you all for the hunt. But you must watch me from a distance. Stay downwind and observe quietly. For hunting, you all need to master patience and observation skills. Watch how I move silently through the Sanctuary, learn how to stalk your prey, and stay vigilant to avoid danger. But remember, always prioritize your safety."

"Got it, Mom!" one cub said excitedly. "We'll be like shadows and watch from afar."

Rani nodded, pride swelling in her chest. "That's my smart cubs. Now, let's practice some stealth movements." She led them through the underbrush, their little bodies mimicking her every move, readying themselves for the wild world that lay ahead.

Chapter 5

The Poachers Threat

The sun had just begun to rise over the horizon, casting a golden hue over the vast expanse of the Ranthambore Wildlife Sanctuary. As the first rays of light filtered through the dense foliage, Rani, the tigress, emerged from her den with a weariness that belied her regal appearance. It had been days without a successful hunt, and it was taking its toll on her once-robust frame, and her ribs were now faintly visible beneath her tawny coat. The pain of hunger only intensified with each passing moment. The summer heat further sapped her energy, and she knew she could no longer ignore the emptiness in her stomach.

With their playful antics and innocent charm, Rani's three cubs were her pride and joy. They relied entirely on her for nourishment, and she dutifully fed them with her milk, which sustained their tiny bodies. However, the constant demands of motherhood left her with little time to replenish her strength.

Determined to provide for her cubs, Rani set out again on a hunt. With a nod to her young ones, she signaled them to stay in the safety of their den while she ventured out during the dusk into the Sanctuary in search of prey. Her senses heightened, and her eyes scanned the surrounding landscape for movement. Her most successful hunts have happened at the pond, where most of her prey visited to quench their thirst.

As she stealthily moved through the dense undergrowth, her ears perked up at the sound of distant gunshots. A chilling sense of unease washed over her as she recognized the familiar sound—the ominous echo of human interference in the Sanctuary. Her instincts told her that danger lurked nearby. The gunshots had set off a wave of panic among the prey, and they scattered in every direction, seeking safety in the labyrinth of the Sanctuary.

Rani crouched low, her muscles tense with apprehension. She could feel the fear rippling through the herd, and her heart pounded with theirs. But amidst the chaos, she spotted something that froze her in her tracks—another tiger, wounded and bleeding, staggering through the underbrush. It was Shashi.

Rani watched with concern and caution as Shashi collapsed 100 feet away from her. The scent of fresh blood hung heavily in the air, mingling with the smell of fear. Poachers were not worried about the GPS collar around Shashi's neck. Poachers have evolved; they can hack into end-of-life GPS devices and accurately locate tigers.

Her first instinct was to approach Shashi to assess the situation. But the distant sound of human footsteps approaching made her reconsider. She knew all too well the threat posed by poachers. She had witnessed other tigers, including cubs, being mercilessly hunted for their valuable skins and bones.

Rani's immediate thought was for the welfare of her cubs. She rushed back to them stealthily without getting seen. She was relieved to see all her cubs back in the den safely. They had perfected Rani's first lessons on staying hidden. Her den was not far away from the poachers. Rani knew she had to act quickly. The safety of her cubs and her own survival was at stake. With a heavy heart, she abandoned her den and relocated to a safer location.

Rani led her cubs away from their familiar den, leaving behind the memories of their first home. Once a place of safety and refuge, the Sanctuary now felt fraught with danger and uncertainty. But Rani's determination to protect her cubs was unwavering, and she pushed forward into the unknown.

Through the unforgiving terrain, she led her young ones to a deeper, more secluded part of the Sanctuary. The dense foliage and towering trees provided a natural fortress, shielding them from prying eyes and potential threats. It was a risky move, but Rani knew that the only chance of survival lay in staying one step ahead of the poachers.

The days turned into weeks, and Rani and her cubs adapted to their new surroundings. They learned to move with stealth and caution, constantly vigilant for signs of danger.

As time passed, the Sanctuary became a battleground, with the ever-present threat of poachers lurking in the shadows. The sound of gunshots became a haunting symphony, a constant reminder of the danger that loomed over them. During these weeks, Rani was very cautious. She avoided going far from her den. This resulted in demand for a proper meal for most of the week. She relied on scavenging and more diminutive, easier prey like turtles and domestic animals.

With each passing day, her cubs grew bolder and more curious about their surroundings. They explored their new territory with wide eyes, taking in the sights and sounds of the wilderness. Rani watched them with a mix of pride and anxiety, knowing that the world they inhabited was both beautiful and unforgiving.

Despite the challenges and the ever-present threat of the poachers, Rani's indomitable spirit shone through. She was a symbol of strength and resilience, a queen of the wild determined to protect her family at any cost. The struggle to survive had forged an unbreakable bond between Rani and her cubs, a bond that would carry them through the darkest of times.

As the sun set over the Sanctuary, casting a warm glow over the landscape, Rani nestled close to her cubs, their bodies entwined in unity and love. The night would bring its challenges, but for now, they found solace in each other's presence.

Chapter 6

A Mother's Dilemma

Most of the time, forest rangers were successful in driving the poachers off, but there were times when the poachers evaded the officials and hunted endangered animals. The echo of gunshots had become a haunting symphony in the Ranthambore Wildlife Sanctuary, a constant reminder of the looming danger that encircled Rani and her vulnerable cubs.

Hunger gnawed at her belly like a relentless predator, driving her to the brink of desperation. The search for sustenance pushed her to the edge, leaving her with no choice but to venture deep into the Sanctuary or move closer to the Sanctuary's boundary, where human settlements were abundant.

The sun hung high, casting its scorching rays upon the arid landscape. As the temperature soared, the Sanctuary's animals sought refuge near water sources, their throats parched, and their bodies fatigued from the unforgiving heat. Rani's instincts, honed by years of survival in the wild, led her to a secluded pond.

However, this man-made pond was close to human settlement.

Her eyes glinted with determination and hunger as she approached the pond. Rani's heart raced with anticipation, and her muscles coiled, ready to unleash the full force of her predatory prowess. She hid herself in the nearby bushes. Her fur was camouflaged with the tall dry bushes.

Unbeknownst to her, a group of shepherds had also sought refuge near the water source, their herd of goats huddled together, seeking respite from the sweltering heat. Rani's sharp senses had been clouded by the gnawing hunger that consumed her, causing her to miss the faint sounds of human chatter carried by the wind. In her weakened state, Rani preferred hunting domestic animals like goats and cows, as they were easier to catch than wild prey.

Her eyes were fixated on goats that were wandering away from the Shepard's safety. In her mind, it was merely a means to an end, an opportunity to satisfy the hunger that unsettled her very core. Unaware of the predator lurking in the shadows, one of the goats drank its fill from the pond and started strolling toward the tall bushes where Rani was hiding. It was oblivious to its impending fate.

With calculated precision, Rani prepared to launch her attack. She had honed her hunting skills through countless battles for survival, and her success rate was a testament to her expertise as a predator. But this time, her calculated ambush would unknowingly lead her to a heartbreaking and unintended consequence.

Rani pounced in a flash of movement, her powerful jaws closing around the goat's neck. The goat bleated in terror, cries for help echoing through the Sanctuary. The other animals scattered in panic, sensing the presence of a predator in their midst. Rani focused solely on her prey, her hunger driving her to overpower the struggling animal.

The shepherds' shouts and cries filled the air as the dust settled. They had witnessed the horrifying sight of their goat being suffocated by Rani. Rani swiftly and effortlessly carried the goat away for half a mile from the scene, and she started feasting on its flesh immediately. She was worried that humans would take back their dead cattle and attack her as well. The shepherds' immediate reaction was one of fear and rage. Rani's ears twitched as she heard the approaching footsteps and voices, but her hunger clouded her judgment, preventing her from sensing the danger now closing in on her.

Two Shepherds' reached the sight where Rani was feasting on their goat. They swung their sticks and threw stones to drive her away without hesitation. Confused and startled, Rani momentarily stopped eating the goat, her instincts turning to self-preservation. She took a few steps back, her eyes locked with those of the shepherds, and she let out a warning growl. But the humans were relentless, driven by the need to protect their livelihood.

Rani's dilemma was stark – should she fight back and risk further provoking the shepherds, or should she retreat and leave the prey she had so desperately sought? Her cubs still depended on her; their safety was her top priority. Yet, hunger still gnawed at her belly, a relentless reminder of the fragile line between survival and desperation.

A hungry tiger would never back down from its hard-earned meal. However, with a heavy heart, Rani retreats, leaving the dead goat behind. Her growls and warning calls echoed through the Sanctuary, reminding the humans she was a force to be reckoned with. Rani was sure the humans would discard the dead goat, and once they left, she could feast on its meat. She stood her ground around 10-15 meters away. Looking at her resolution, these two shepherds followed Rani and threw stones at her. Rani backed up a few meters. This gave the two shepherds more confidence, and they followed her deeper into the forest. She ran back some more, but the shepherds continued their pursuit. She was close to her den and cubs.

This was getting dangerous for her. She knew that if the shepherds followed her to the den, her cubs would be slaughtered. She decided to put up a fight. She pounced on one of the shepherds, held him down with her forelimbs, and grabbed his throat with her massive canines. The other shepherd was in shock and could not muster the strength to confront her. He shouted for others to help. The loud sound echoed for miles.

The rest of the shepherds weren't far behind; within minutes, they arrived, brandishing long wooden sticks. Now, five or six more shepherds came to the scene. Rani decided to back down and save herself. She let the shepherd free, whose throat she was biting down on. Tigers do not know restraint. They always have the intent to kill. The shepherd was not breathing anymore. Despite the numerous respiratory revival efforts, the rest of the shepherds put in, he remained motionless. He was immediately picked up and carried by the group.

The enraged shepherds decided to take revenge on the tigress by poisoning the carcass of the dead goat. They hoped Rani would take the bait, but she did not return to the area again. Tragically, a leopard and some vultures consumed the poisoned carcass that same day, resulting in their instant deaths.

This encounter had left a bitter taste in Rani's mouth, a reminder of the harsh reality of life in the wild. The

Sanctuary, intended to be a safe haven for the creatures it housed, had become a battleground of survival, where the needs of humans and animals collided in a heartbreaking dance of life and death.

Chapter 7

A Desperate Escape

As the day dawned, casting its golden glow upon the Sanctuary, the news of the dead shepherd reached the ears of the villagers and the forest rangers. The unfortunate man's relatives, distraught by his sudden death, sought help from the poachers, the very individuals responsible for causing turmoil and chaos in the once tranquil Sanctuary. The shepherds shared Rani's last location with the poachers.

As dusk settled, the poachers, driven by insatiable greed and a blatant disregard for the consequences, quickly responded to the call for help. Sensing an opportunity to exploit the situation, they devised a plan to sedate the tigress with tranquilizer guns and capture her cubs alive. To them, these majestic creatures were merely pawns in their ruthless game, with the expectation that the missing cubs would soon be forgotten. Whether dead or alive, Rani was to be their consolation prize, as her skin, teeth, and bones would fetch a high market value. They intended to act immediately, hoping to secure their prize before the forest rangers could intervene and thwart their plans.

With a sense of malevolence and excitement, the six poachers with rifles and tranquilizer guns ventured into the heart of the Sanctuary, their eyes gleaming with the promise of a lucrative bounty. They knew capturing the cubs alone would fetch a handsome price on the black market, and their minds were blinded by the prospect of material gain. Once a refuge for these endangered animals, the Sanctuary became a battleground of greed and betrayal.

Meanwhile, Rani was unaware of the unfolding events. She was keeping a watchful eye on her cubs as they played and frolicked in the safety of their den. Her maternal instincts were at their peak, and her heart swelled with love and protection for her young ones. But her senses were heightened, and she could sense the impending danger that lurked nearby.

In the pitch dark, the poachers headed to Rani's last known location, evading the cameras placed by the forest rangers. Forest rangers conducted scheduled patrols of the wildlife in the forest every night. Poachers were aware of these schedules and were wise to avoid confrontations.

The poachers were now almost a mile away from the den. As they crept closer, their stealth was betrayed by the rustling of leaves underfoot. Rani's instincts kicked into overdrive. Her ears twitched, catching the faintest sounds of human presence. A growl rumbled in her throat, warning the unseen intruders that she was aware of their presence and prepared to defend her cubs at any cost.

In a split-second decision, fueled by her fierce love for her offspring, Rani made a choice that would shape the fate of her family. Her heart pounded in her chest as she gathered her cubs close. The air was thick with tension, and her eyes glinted with determination.

"Listen to me carefully, my little ones," Rani whispered urgently, her voice a mix of fierce love and concern. "You must stay silent and hidden deep in our den. Don't venture out for any reason. Mommy will carry one of you at a time and take you to our new den."

One of the cubs, eyes wide with worry, asked, "But why do we have to hide, Mom?"

Rani licked the cub's forehead gently. "Humans are nearby, my love. They can be very dangerous. We must not let them find you all."

Another cub, with a tremor in its voice, questioned, "What if they come here, Mom? What should we do?"

Rani's gaze hardened. "Stay as quiet as the night. They must not hear or see you."

"Will you be back soon, Mom? What if something happens to you?"

Rani's heart ached, but she stood firm. "I promise I'll return as quickly as I can. You all are strong and brave, just like your mother. Trust in your instincts and stay together. We'll get through this."

With one last lingering look at her precious cubs, Rani picked one cub in her jaw and slipped silently into the underbrush. The other two cubs watched her go, their young hearts pounding with a mix of fear and admiration. They knew their mother was fierce and wise, and they clung to her words, hoping for her swift return.

As Rani moved stealthily through the jungle, every sense was on high alert. She knew the risks but had to find a safer place for her family. The echoes of her promise to her cubs fueled her determination as she ventured deeper into the wild, driven by a mother's unyielding love and the fierce instinct to protect her young.

She had decided to venture back into the deep forest, not worrying about intruding into another tiger's territory. As she ran, her powerful muscles propelled her through the dense undergrowth. Rani felt a surge of both fear and determination. She knew that leaving her other cubs behind was a painful sacrifice, but she also knew that she had to ensure the safety of at least one of them.

It is growing more difficult each day to find a new hiding place with the rise of human encroachment and rampant deforestation. Rani returned to her mother's old hiding spot, a place she had inherited as her own territory. This location was a safe distance from her previous den. Her heart was heavy, knowing her other cubs were now vulnerable to poachers' traps. Tears welled in her eyes as she gently set the cub down, nuzzling it lovingly before taking one last look back at the new den. 'Stay here, my brave cub. I will bring your brother and sister soon.' It was a farewell filled with anguish and sorrow.

As she retraced her steps back to the old den, her senses on high alert, Rani's worst fears were realized. The poachers had descended upon the old den, their cruel intentions laid bare as they captured her two defenseless cubs and put them in small rectangular metal cages that would barely fit two four-month-old tiger cubs. The sight was enough to make her blood boil with rage, and her heart pounded with the fierce determination to rescue her young ones from the clutches of these heartless predators.

The poachers, emboldened by their success, laughed callously as they secured the cubs in crude cages, their eyes glinting with malicious satisfaction. The once-vibrant and playful young ones now trembled in fear, their innocence stolen from them by the cruel hand of fate. The cubs continuously called out for Rani in their feeble and scared roar. Rani could not bear to witness their suffering, her motherly instincts urging her to act and rescue her cubs from this nightmarish fate.

With a guttural roar that shook the very foundation of the Sanctuary, Rani launched her attack. Her eyes blazed with fiery intensity; her determination unwavering as she charged toward the poachers with the force of a tempest. The poachers, caught off guard by the ferocity and speed of her assault, scrambled to defend themselves against the enraged tigress.

In a whirlwind of claws and teeth, Rani fought with primal fury, her mind solely focused on rescuing her cubs. The poachers, taken aback by her unwavering resolve, tried to subdue her with tranquilizers, but their efforts were in vain against the indomitable spirit of the tigress. With only three LED torches flickering between them, the poachers were ill-equipped to pinpoint Rani's location in the dense darkness. Rani had the advantage of the night and the tall grass on her side. Although enraged, she was not careless. She knew it was best to launch a surprise attack from their blind spots rather than a head-on attack, resulting in the poachers getting a good headshot.

Rani was able to severely hurt three of the poachers. Her sharp claws, backed by powerful brute strength, severely damaged them. Some lost fingers, while others dislocated their shoulders and bled profusely. In a desperate bid to escape her wrath, the three injured poachers managed to flee from the scene, leaving their remaining three comrades behind to bear the brunt of Rani's fury. The tigress was relentless, her determination unyielding as she fought tooth and claw to free her young ones from the cruel captivity that had befallen them.

The remaining three poachers had only one torch among them, which was insufficient to illuminate the entire area. The cage holding the cubs was left unattended as well. Rani took this opportunity and leveraged the darkness to stealthily snatch the cage. She dismantled the cage's door with a mighty swipe of her paw. However, she could only free one of her cubs in a moment of triumphant victory. The little one scurried to her side, seeking solace and protection in the comforting embrace of its mother. The second caged cub had its leg stuck in the cage's metal rod. Rani and the second cub tried hard to set free but were unsuccessful. She was losing precious time.

The three poachers seized the moment to regroup. They switched from tranquilizer guns to rifles loaded with live rounds, attaching suppressors to avoid alerting the forest rangers. Their goal was no longer to capture the tigress alive. As they began firing, the live rounds instilled panic and fear in Rani. She retreated, seeking refuge behind the nearest tall grass, and leaving both her cubs behind. Aware of the imminent danger, Rani knew she had to avoid confrontation to preserve her life.

The poachers continued shooting in her direction, and one bullet grazed her right forelimb. Taking advantage of the chaos, the poachers quickly seized the cub that had been freed and shoved it into the broken cage. They secured the cage with ropes to prevent any escape. Not waiting for Rani to counterattack, they fled the scene on foot, leaving her wounded and desperate.

Rani was bleeding from the bullet wound, but this did not faze her at all. The battle was far from over, and Rani knew that she had to press on, that the fate of both her cubs still hung in the balance. With a heart-heavy determination and love, she licked her wounds and set out on a desperate pursuit of the poachers, her eyes locked on the trail they had left behind. The poachers had an excellent one-mile lead on her.

Through the unforgiving terrain of the Sanctuary, Rani chased after the poachers, her heart racing with fear and hope. Her breath came in ragged gasps, but she refused to let exhaustion deter her from the rescue mission. Her fierce love for her cubs fueled her every step, and she knew she could not rest until her young ones were safely by her side again.

Rani had no idea where the poachers were headed, but she knew she had to keep going because her cubs' lives depended on her unwavering resolve. She was able to follow the cries of her cubs. With each passing moment, Rani's resolve grew more pungent, her spirit undaunted by her hardships. The Sanctuary had become a battleground; she was a fearless guardian, fighting against the forces that sought to tear her family apart.

The night stretched on, and the Sanctuary was shrouded in darkness. But within the depths of that darkness, a mother's love burned brightly, guiding Rani through the treacherous path before her. The poachers had underestimated the power of a mother's love and gravely underestimated the tigress's strength and determination.

As the night deepened, Rani's determination bore fruit. She tracked the poachers to their temporary camp within the Sanctuary. They had holed up, hoping to evade her relentless pursuit. Filled with a mix of fear and anticipation, Rani prepared for the confrontation. Her heart pounded with the knowledge that her cubs were so close, within her reach once more.

Chapter 8

Relentless Pursuit

The night had brought a renewed sense of purpose, and the tigress was ready to take on the poachers who had dared to separate her from her precious cubs. The Sanctuary echoed with the sounds of the wilderness, but amidst the symphony of nature, a battle was about to unfold, fueled by a mother's love and a thirst for vengeance.

With stealth and precision, Rani planned her attack. She knew the poachers would be on high alert, expecting her to come for her cubs. But she also knew that the night offered her an advantage – the element of surprise. The darkness was her ally, concealing her movements as she stalked the poachers from the shadows.

Her heart pounded in her chest with every step, a rhythmic drumbeat of determination and adrenaline. Her senses were heightened, attuned to every sound and scent that lingered in the air. She could hear the faint rustle of leaves, the soft footfalls of the poachers, and the rapid beating of her heart as she prepared to face the danger ahead.

Rani moved like a ghost in the night, her form blending seamlessly with the surrounding darkness. Unaware of her presence, the poachers were focused on exiting the forest, which was hardly a matter of a few miles. But they had to ensure they evade the forest rangers guarding the forest boundaries.

With a low growl that reverberated through the stillness of the night, Rani made her presence known. The poachers were taken aback, their hearts quickening with fear as they realized they were no longer the hunters but the hunted. Panic spread like wildfire among them, and they fumbled to locate the source of the menacing growl that had shattered the silence.

In the pitch dark, the poachers resorted to desperate measures. They fired from their noise-suppressed rifles in all directions, but the veil of darkness impaired their aim, and most of their shots missed their mark. Rani used the tall grass nearby to her advantage, stealthily moving around, avoiding the barrage of bullets that whizzed through the air. The poachers were not able to pinpoint her exact hiding spot.

In the random shooting, one of the bullets found its target. Pain seared through Rani's left hind leg, but she refused to yield. Her love for her cubs burned brighter than the pain that threatened to slow her down. With every ounce of strength she had left, she pressed on, her eyes locked on the poachers, her determination unwavering.

Sensing their prey was wounded but not defeated, the poachers regrouped and devised a new defense plan. They knew they had to subdue the tigress to escape with their lives intact. They decided to scare the angry tigress with fire. They swiftly ignited a few logs using an alcohol-soaked cloth and a cigarette lighter, tools they always carry with them. They threw these logs in different directions. Animals are cautious around the fire. They prefer to avoid this element of nature. Some are extremely scared. The fire took Rani by surprise. She stood her ground as the fire spread in all directions around their camp.

For a few tense minutes, the poachers lost track of Rani's presence. Suddenly, she leaped through the fire, landing on an unsuspecting poacher with her powerful jaws and razor-sharp claws. She fought with primal fury, her eyes blazing with fierce determination that sent shivers down the spines of her adversaries. She grabbed one of the poachers by his waist, her mighty claws digging deep into his stomach, then bit his neck from behind. This all happened in a matter of seconds, leaving the poacher frozen in his tracks, unable to resist the overwhelming force of the tigress. Rani's growl, while holding the poacher's neck, sent chills down the spines of the remaining two poachers.

Amid the chaos, the remaining two poachers realized they were no match for the tigress's relentless onslaught. Fear gripped their hearts, and they knew they had to return to the village, where they could get more help. The two remaining poachers grabbed the cage and ran for the forest boundary, leaving behind the Sanctuary that had become a battlefield. Rani released the poacher from her grasp only after confirming he was no longer breathing.

Chapter 9

Trapped

The poachers cunningly returned to their base village, dragging the helpless cubs along. Luck was on their side as they missed the forest rangers patrolling the forest boundary. With some angry and vengeful villagers on their side, they soon changed their plan to a more calculated and sinister one. They thought of using the innocent cubs as bait to capture and dispatch Rani, and sell her remains in the lucrative black market outside India. It was a scheme born out of greed and disregard for the sacredness of life, a testament to the depths of human depravity.

Meanwhile, Rani stealthily trailed the poachers and the cries of her cubs, determined to rescue her cubs from their clutches. Her motherly instincts pushed her forward even as the odds stacked against her. She knew the danger that awaited her, but her love for her young ones propelled her forward, her eyes blazing with fierce determination.

A sense of foreboding washed over her as she closed in on the poachers' location. Her wounds were slowing her speed. She had to take a pause, lick her wounds, and then carry on again. Her love for her cubs outweighed her pain, and she pressed on, her powerful muscles propelling her forward with unmatched grace.

The poachers had immediately set a cunning pitfall trap for Rani. They covered a Fifteen-foot-deep well with a light surface made of branches and leaves, appearing to be solid ground that masked the danger lurking beneath. This light surface would not stand the weight of a Tiger. The well had at least 5 feet of residual water in it. The well had no fence around its opening. The cage with tiger cubs was then carefully suspended from a nearby tree branch and placed right on top of this light surface. The idea was that as soon as Rani approached the cage with the cubs, her heavy weight would make her fall into the well. Since tigers are good swimmers, she wouldn't drown. This meant the poachers had a good chance of trapping and killing a beast.

After an hour of setting up the trap, Rani arrived at the scene, her eyes scanning her surroundings. She sensed nothing amiss; no humans were in sight. The two poachers were hiding in the hut nearby. They ensured the area's lights were turned off. This would make Rani careless and would easily approach the trap. However, Rani was being very cautious of her surroundings. The cubs, joyous to see their mother, roared even more. When Rani approached the well, she smelled the pitfall. Tigers have a keen sense; she could easily smell the water underneath. However, her judgment was clouded by the maternal instinct to save her young cubs.

She placed one of her front legs on the light surface; however, nothing happened. She gained more confidence. She stepped further; more than half of her body was now on top of this pitfall. The light surface could no longer hold this massive cat, and the ground beneath her gave way. Soon, she found herself plummeting 15 feet into the depths of the well. Panic surged through her. She growled and tried numerous times to climb the wall. Poachers turned on the lights of the area.

Rani tried to grasp the wall but could not leap out of the well and fell back to the bottom. She fought to stay composed, knowing she needed to escape the deadly trap if she had any hope of saving her cubs.

The poachers heaved a sigh of relief, their faces twisted with cruel glee, as they approached the trench, ready to capture the tigress alive. They had tranquilizers ready, a means to subdue her and prevent her from putting up a fight. But they underestimated Rani's strength and resilience.

Rani was losing blood from her wound as well, but there was no time to think about it. While she gathered her strength and caught her breath, the poachers stood poised with their rifles and Rani squarely in their rifle's crosshairs.

In the dark, it was difficult to aim Rani's head. They aimlessly shot twice at her visible body. Unfortunately, the bullets could not penetrate deep into her back, as it was submerged underwater. The water created some resistance, reducing the bullet's velocity. Still, it had some impact on her. Now, she was bleeding from her back as well. Rani started feeling numbness in her lower body and felt disoriented as well.

In that moment of stillness, she ceased her agitation and carefully surveyed the well, identifying a potential ledge that could offer a foothold for her escape. The poachers and villagers, mistaking her motionless state for impending death, believed they would soon be able to haul her out with ropes and began to relax, already counting their future earnings. Meanwhile, Rani was gathering all her strength, preparing for a mighty leap to free herself from the well.

This happy moment for the poachers lasted seconds as Rani lunged out of the well with all her strength. Tigers are known for their agility and strength and are capable climbers. They can easily climb trees up to 15 feet tall. The mere sight of her made everyone freeze where they stood. Despite losing focus, Rani leaped and pounced on one of them, her claws slashing through the darkness like fiery blades.

One poacher lay lifeless on the ground in the chaos that ensued, their schemes undone by the tigress's bravery. Rani attacked two villagers, mauling them badly and leaving them bleeding. The wrath of the wild was unleashed upon them. The rest of the villagers fled to their huts, abandoning the sole poacher to fend for himself. Rani's fury knew no bounds as she fought to protect herself and her cubs from the heartless predators. But even the most tenacious warriors can be brought down.

The last poacher was having an alignment issue with his suppressor. The poacher decided to get rid of his suppressor in order to avoid baffle strikes. Baffle strike refers to a malfunction caused when the fired bullet hits the internal parts of the suppressor. Rani's moment of triumph was short-lived. A loud thud echoed through the air as she moved to finish off the last remaining poacher. In an instant, she collapsed and lay motionless. The final poacher had shot her in the head. Her vision blurred, and the world around her faded into darkness. Her heart ached with a sense of betrayal, knowing that her valiant efforts had ultimately led to her death.

The gunshot was loud, alarming the nearby forest rangers. The poacher knew he had probably 20 minutes before the forest rangers would arrive at this spot. He paid some of the villagers handsomely to assist him in skinning Rani. In a matter of 15 minutes, they skinned her quickly, pulled out her teeth, broke some bones, hacked her legs, and threw the undesirable body parts in the well. All this unfolded right in front of Rani's 2 cubs.

With his nefarious mission accomplished, the poacher wasted no time escaping. His greed had prevailed, and he had claimed his reward – the magnificent Rani, reduced to nothing more than a commodity to be traded in the world's dark corners. The poacher made a run with Rani's remains and her two cubs using his old wagon. In the next few hours, he called many interested parties and made deals with the highest bidder. Rani's carcass was finalized to be sold to the highest Chinese bidder. The carcass would be cautiously moved to China via Nepal. He also found a middleman who would pay him handsomely for Rani's 2 cubs.

Chapter 10

The Cubs Fate

The following week, the poacher delivered the two cubs to the nearest port in Rajasthan. The cubs were now being smuggled by hiding them inside a legitimate cargo. He received hefty cash as a reward, which would feed his family of four for the next ten years. A European middleman trafficking the cubs never informed him about the destination for relocating the cubs. The middleman had planned to place the cubs in a zoo in Washington D.C., United States of America.

The journey to the USA zoo had been long and arduous. The cubs arrived after a month-long sea voyage. The sights, smells, and sounds were foreign, starkly contrasting the familiar territory of their Sanctuary in Ranthambore. As the cubs arrived in the United States, the two cubs' spirits were broken, but the weight of captivity bore heavily upon them. They were placed in warm confines and were scared as they could hear sounds made by different animals and birds, which they had never heard before.

It was not long before made-up news circulated in the USA that a captive royal Bengal tigress had died while giving birth in a USA Zoo. Her two cubs were now raised by hardworking zookeepers and fed by other non-predatory mammals. Videos surfaced on social media platforms showing how kind humans and other animals care for orphaned extinct animals. However, we know the real story of these unfortunate cubs. The zoo also gave them names; the older male was called Nash, and the female sibling was called Izzy.

The cubs separation from their mother and loss of their natural habitat were jarring and bewildering. They had been robbed of the chance to learn from their mother, explore the wild, and develop the skills necessary for survival.

In this USA zoo, visitors marveled at the sight of Nash and Izzy, ignorant of the pain and anguish behind those innocent faces. To them, the cubs were merely entertainment, a means to pass the time and marvel at the exotic creatures. But beneath the surface, the cubs yearned for the embrace of their mother and the vastness of the wilderness they had never known.

This zoo did not have any other tigers for their company. They had to grow alongside the lions. The lions never accepted these orphaned cubs. The two cubs' growth was linear; however, their once playful antics were replaced by a more subdued demeanor. They had lost the spark of life that once defined them, their spirits dampened by the confines of their enclosures. They were shadows of the wild creatures they were meant to be, their heritage and instincts suppressed by the artificiality of their new homes. All they had was each other; a queen's blood rushed through them. They were made to outlast all obstacles, and they did the same.

After 6 months, they showed signs of recovery and were on the path to becoming the children of The Queen of Ranthambore.

On the other hand, thousands of miles back in India, in the vast expanse of the Ranthambore Wildlife Sanctuary, news of Rani's poaching incident spread the same day. A team of dedicated wildlife conservationists, along with forest Rangers, embarked on a mission to rescue the surviving cubs of Rani.

These individuals were driven by a deep sense of responsibility and a commitment to protecting their nation's precious wildlife. They were determined to right the wrongs that had befallen Rani and her cubs.

The rescue operation had its challenges. Finally, after great efforts, the third cub was located three days after his separation from Rani. The cub, separated from its mother and siblings, was disoriented, scared, and hungry. The forest rangers approached cautiously, aware of the cub's instincts and the possibility of it lashing out in fear. But the team's compassion and expertise prevailed as they gently coaxed the cub into a specialized transport crate, ensuring its safety during the journey to its new temporary home.

The animal shelter selected to host the cub was not just any ordinary facility; it was a sanctuary of hope and rehabilitation for rescued wildlife. Nestled amidst lush greenery and sprawling grounds, the shelter was designed to replicate the natural habitat of the creatures it housed, offering them a semblance of the freedom they were meant to enjoy.

Upon arrival at the shelter, the cub was greeted by a team of caring and experienced caregivers. Their hearts were heavy with the knowledge of the cub's painful past, but they were resolute in their commitment to provide the best possible care and support. This cub was named "Sundar," meaning beautiful in Hindi.

In the early days, Sundar kept to itself, wary of the new environment and the presence of humans. The caregivers knew healing would take time and patience, so they allowed Sundar space to acclimate. Caregivers had identified a surrogate Tiger mother for this third cub. Trust began to bloom slowly but steadily between the cub and its new family.

A team of dedicated veterinarians conducted a thorough health assessment, addressing Sundar's physical injuries and providing essential medical care.

The veterinarians were relieved to find that the injury was not severe. With proper rest and treatment, the cub began to heal, a testament to the resilience of these magnificent creatures.

As the days turned into weeks, Sundar's transformation was miraculous. The once timid and fearful creature grew in strength and confidence. The lush surroundings and the gentle care provided by the shelter staff allowed the cub to flourish.

The shelter's philosophy was rooted in the belief that every creature deserved to live a life of dignity and freedom. Sundar was provided ample space to roam, climb, and explore, and the caregivers observed with joy as the young one rediscovered the pleasure of being wild.

It was heartwarming to witness the cub's playful antics, a stark contrast to the fear and helplessness it had experienced not long ago. The shelter's mission was to provide a temporary refuge and prepare the cub for a future where it could thrive in the wild once again.

Sundar's rehabilitation included honing its hunting skills, which are critical for survival in the wild. Caregivers provided the cub with opportunities to practice stalking, pouncing, and capturing prey, skills passed down through generations but disrupted by the trauma of captivity.

In addition to developing physical capabilities, Sundar was also introduced to other rescued animals, fostering social interactions vital for its well-being. Bonds formed between the young tiger and fellow shelter inhabitants, creating a sense of community and camaraderie that mirrored the social dynamics of tigers in the wild.

As time passed, the young tiger's transformation was remarkable. The once vulnerable and disoriented creature had become a symbol of hope and resilience. Its spirit had been rekindled, and the indomitable tiger essence burned brightly within its soul.

With each passing day, the bond between Sundar and its caregivers deepened. The humans who had saved the young one from the clutches of captivity had become surrogate parents, guardians guiding the young tiger toward its eventual return to the wild.

The shelter's ultimate goal was to reintroduce Sundar to its natural habitat, a goal that was no small feat. Before Sundar could be set free, extensive preparations were undertaken to ensure its safety and success in the wild.

The shelter collaborated with renowned experts in tiger conservation to devise a comprehensive plan for Sundar's reintroduction. They decided that Sundar and others like him would be released once they were almost 24 months old. It involved closely monitoring the cub's progress, simulating natural hunting scenarios, and gradually expanding the area of its enclosure to mimic the expansive territories tigers would roam in the wild.

As the day of Sundar's release approached, the shelter staff's emotions ran high. They knew that the day would mark the culmination of their tireless efforts, but it was also bittersweet, as they had grown deeply attached to the young one they had nurtured.

On the release day, the shelter staff gathered with heavy hearts, knowing they were about to say goodbye to the cub they had come to love like family. But they also knew that this was the moment the cub had been waiting for when it could return to the freedom and wilderness it was destined for. Sundar was fitted with the latest state-of-the-art GPS tracker to monitor its movement and understand the tiger's behavior in the wild.

Amidst the lush vegetation of Ranthambore, the shelter staff carefully opened the door of the transport crate. For a moment, Sundar hesitated, its keen senses taking in the sights and sounds of its familiar surroundings.

And then, with a burst of energy and determination, Sundar stepped out of the crate and onto the soft Earth of the Sanctuary. It took a few cautious steps, its eyes filled with wonder and excitement. And then, as if sensing the call of its ancestors, Sundar broke into a run, its powerful muscles propelling it forward.

The shelter staff watched with tear-filled eyes as Sundar disappeared into the wilderness, its golden coat blending seamlessly with the vibrant hues of the forest. It was a moment of both loss and triumph, symbolizing these magnificent creatures' resilience and the power of compassion and dedication.

The fate of the last cub had been transformed from one of darkness and captivity to one of freedom and possibility. The shelter that had provided solace and rehabilitation to this young one continued its mission, tirelessly working to protect and preserve the majestic creatures of the wild.

In a world where tigers faced numerous threats, the story of the last cub was a testament to humanity's power to make a difference. It was a reminder that even in the face of overwhelming challenges, hope could shine through, illuminating a path of compassion, respect, and preservation for these magnificent creatures and the wilderness they called home.

Chapter 11

The Unforgotten Tragedy

The poacher carrying Rani's carcass was caught in northern India near the Nepal border. The carcass was recovered, and the poacher was interrogated. He detailed the entire incident to the local police officials. However, since he lacked detailed information about the European middleman, the Indian officials could not recover the lost two cubs. Based on his information, forest officials installed more surveillance cameras to cover the blind spots described by the poacher. An additional team was hired to protect the Sanctuary around the clock. Neighboring villagers were warned not to entertain poachers, or they would face the same legal consequences as the poachers themselves for aiding them, or worse, they would be forced to relocate.

Rani was a famous tiger, and her sudden disappearance did not go unnoticed. Many news channels speculated that she had been killed by another tiger over territory or poisoned by villagers. However, the true story soon emerged and spread like wildfire. The recovered carcass was brought back to Ranthambore and was given a royal cremation, which was highly publicized. This led to widespread criticism of the forest officials.

The final chapter of Rani's story unfolded with bittersweet resonance. Filled with bravery and sacrifice, her tale evoked emotions akin to those stirred by epic sagas of human triumphs and tribulations. But Rani was not human; she was a tigress, a wild creature whose struggles and resilience had largely gone unnoticed by the world.

In a world where sensational human stories often dominated headlines and captured global attention, the plight of majestic creatures like Rani usually remained relegated to the periphery of public consciousness. The tragedy that unfolded in the wilderness of Ranthambore was a blunt reminder of humanity's indifference to the suffering of other species, a poignant reflection of how easily the lives and struggles of non-human beings could be overlooked.

As a tigress, Rani embodied the untamed spirit of the wild, which ancient civilizations revered and celebrated. But with time, humanity's relationship with nature has profoundly shifted. The once revered creatures of the wild have become victims of greed and exploitation, their lives reduced to commodities in a cruel and unyielding trade.

The poaching and illegal trade in wildlife had far-reaching consequences, not just for individual creatures like Rani but for entire ecosystems. As apex predators, tigers play a critical role in maintaining the delicate balance of nature. Their presence helps regulate the populations of prey species, which in turn influences vegetation and other wildlife. Losing a single tiger had ripple effects that could disrupt the ecological equilibrium.

Yet, despite the gravity of the situation, the plight of these majestic creatures often remained overlooked. While passionate wildlife conservationists and dedicated organizations worked tirelessly to protect them, their efforts were usually overshadowed by other pressing issues.

It is a call to address the root causes of poaching, such as poverty and lack of alternative livelihoods for communities living near wildlife sanctuaries. By providing sustainable livelihood options and involving local communities in conservation efforts, reducing the incentives for poaching, and fostering a sense of ownership and pride in preserving wildlife was possible.

The call for compassion also extends to consumer behavior. A global market fueled the demand for wildlife products in the black market, and consumers needed to be aware of the consequences of their choices. By shunning products made from endangered species and opting for sustainable alternatives, individuals could make a significant impact in curbing the illegal wildlife trade.

Awareness plays a vital role in fostering compassion and understanding. By incorporating wildlife conservation into school curricula and raising awareness through public campaigns, it is possible to instill a sense of stewardship for the natural world in the younger generation.

Beyond the Story

Facts and Figures

In the early 20th century, the tiger population in Asia stood robustly at an estimated 100,000 individuals. However, as we entered the 21st century, this once-thriving population had plummeted to fewer than 5000, marking a staggering decline of over 95% in less than a century. This precipitous decrease can be predominantly attributed to rampant hunting, encompassing legal and illegal practices, driven by the historical perception of tigers as prestigious symbols and coveted trophies for big-game hunters.

Throughout history, tigers have been revered for their majestic aura, and their body parts have been sought for various purposes. The demand for tiger skins, bones, and organs has perpetuated a devastating cycle of hunting, posing an imminent threat to their survival. Unfortunately, tigers find themselves ensnared in the trade of traditional Asian medicine and luxury goods and as symbols of status, further exacerbating the challenges to their existence.

While the past few decades have witnessed positive strides, such as heightened anti-poaching efforts and dedicated conservation initiatives, the tiger population remains critically low. As of 2022, conservative estimates indicate that approximately 5,574 wild tigers endure, with discernible regional variations in population trends.

Tiger habitats face additional pressures from human activities, including logging, agriculture, and infrastructure development. These vital habitats' consequential destruction and fragmentation contribute significantly to the ongoing decline in tiger populations. Efforts to preserve and restore these ecosystems are paramount to securing the future of these iconic big cats.

Global and local endeavors are crucial for the conservation and protection of tigers. The fragile state of these magnificent creatures underscores the urgency of addressing issues such as habitat loss, poaching, and the illegal wildlife trade. Despite these odds, there is hope to reverse the alarming decline and secure a more optimistic future for the world's remaining wild tigers only through concerted international collaboration, sustained anti-poaching measures, and comprehensive conservation strategies.

Story 2

Maternal Devotion

Chapter 1

Phil's World

Once upon a time, in the vast and shimmering Pacific Ocean, where the waters stretched to seemingly infinite horizons, there lived a mischievous sperm whale named Phil. The ocean was his playground, a vast expanse of azure waves dancing beneath the radiant sun, creating a breathtaking backdrop for Phil's adventures. He would glide through the gentle waves, leaping playfully into the air and sending sparkling droplets cascading like diamonds in the sunlight. Phil's days were filled with joy and curiosity as he explored the wonders of his oceanic home.

Phil was a young and spirited whale, full of life and vigor. Having recently celebrated his first birthday, he had already grown to a length of almost 15 feet, an impressive size for his age. Yet, compared to his mother, Rose, he was still just a playful calf. Rose was a majestic and healthy whale, twenty years old, and an experienced mother. At an impressive 35 feet in length, she commanded respect and admiration from the entire pod.

The pod was a close-knit family with twelve females, including Rose, and four adorable calves. They were bound together by strong bonds of love and companionship and navigated the vast ocean as one cohesive unit.

Rose was the heart and soul of the pod, the matriarch who led them with wisdom and grace. She had seen the ocean through her mother's eyes, who had passed down stories and traditions that enriched the pod's lives. The tales were woven with legends of the past, experiences from generations before, and insights into the wonders and dangers that lay beyond their watery home.

Rose's stories with the pod painted a vivid picture of the oceanic world. They spoke of breathtaking underwater landscapes, vibrant coral reefs, and the dazzling array of marine life that coexisted in harmony. Yet, they also warned of the lurking dangers, the treacherous predators that inhabited the depths, and the harsh realities of their existence. The ocean was a realm of wonder and mystery, where beauty and peril were intertwined.

As Phil listened to his mother's stories, his young mind was filled with wonder and awe. He yearned to explore the ocean's hidden treasures and uncover its secrets. Rose's tales ignited a curiosity within him, urging him to venture further into the vast blue beyond.

However, amidst the marvels of the ocean, Rose never shied away from revealing the harsh truth about the threats that loomed over their lives. Among the most formidable adversaries were relentless humans who hunted whales for various purposes. Whaling, as it was called, was a cruel practice that had caused immense suffering and led to a significant depletion of whale populations.

Rose recounted her encounter with whalers as a calf, the memory etched in her heart with pain and sorrow. She explained how the humans would approach whales in large ships armed with deadly weapons. The sharp projectiles would be launched at the unsuspecting whales, exploding upon impact, and inflicting unimaginable agony. Rose was referring to harpoons having explosives at its tip. The sea would turn red with blood, and the cries of the wounded would echo through the waters.

Humans sought whales for their valuable resources, hunting them for their meat, which is considered a delicacy in many regions. Sperm whale oil is highly valued for its high quality and versatility. This oil is extracted from the spermaceti organ in their head. It was used in lamps, lubricants, candles, and cosmetics. Even whale excrement, known as ambergris, is highly prized. Often referred to as the "treasure of the sea" or "floating gold," ambergris is a rare, natural byproduct of the sperm whale's squid-based diet.

From ambergris, an odorless alcohol called ambrein is extracted, which is used to make a perfume's scent last longer. In some cultures, ambergris has been used for medicinal purposes, believed to offer various health benefits, although these uses are not widely supported by modern science. Historically, ambergris has also been considered an aphrodisiac in certain cultures. Ambergris is one of the most expensive natural substances on the market, selling for approximately $20,000 to $50,000 per kilogram, depending on its quality.

The cruelty of the whaling practice has weighed heavily on Rose's heart. She has always stressed on the importance of cherishing every life and acknowledging the interconnectedness of all living beings within their ecosystem.

Still a young calf, Phil tried to comprehend the gravity of his mother's words. He could sense the pain in her voice, the sorrow that resonated from the depths of her soul. Rose's teachings about the human threat were both a cautionary tale and a testament to the resilience of their species.

As time passed, Phil thrived, his strength and size increasing exponentially. Swimming alongside his mother, he marveled at the ocean's wonders, the coral reefs' vibrant colors, and the schools of fish dancing in synchrony. Every sunrise brought a new day of exploration and discovery.

Rose, the wise matriarch, guided her son through the intricacies of life in the ocean. She taught him how to communicate with the pod through a symphony of clicks, enabling them to stay connected even across vast distances. These clicks are also used to scare other predators. Sperm whales can generate extremely loud clicks, reaching up to 230 decibels. This is one of the loudest sounds produced by any mammal and can travel for miles underwater.

The bond between mother and calf grew stronger with each passing day as Rose instilled in Phil the values of love, compassion, and unity. Phil would always nestle close to his mother, seeking comfort and warmth in her embrace. In the silence of the deep ocean, she would tell him more stories, stories of bravery and courage, unity, and perseverance. Phil would listen with rapt attention, his imagination soaring with every word.

As Phil approached his second birthday, he had grown into a curious and adventurous young whale. He relished the freedom of the open ocean, where he could explore the depths and soar to the surface, breaching with exuberance. Each day brought new experiences, encounters with marine creatures, and a growing understanding of the delicate balance of life in the ocean. He knew the sea was also a place of vulnerability with all its beauty and majesty. He felt a sense of responsibility to protect his pod and their way of life, just as Rose had done before him.

Little did he know that the trials he would face and the choices he would shape his destiny. As the currents of fate carried him forward, Phil would learn the true meaning of courage, sacrifice, and the enduring power of love in the face of adversity. His journey had only begun, and the ocean held endless possibilities for a young whale with a heart full of wonder and a soul yearning for adventure.

Chapter 2

Tales of the Pod

Rose's pod was like a close-knit family, with twelve wise and caring females, including Rose, who formed a harmonious group. The pod members had a deep bond built on trust and nurtured through the generations. Their seamless coordination and cooperation allowed them to navigate the ever-changing currents of the ocean with grace and ease. During the austral summer months, from December to March, the pod migrates to the Southern Ocean for an abundant food supply, primarily Squid and Krill.

Within the pod were four adorable calves, including Phil, who was the essence of innocence and curiosity. They swam alongside their mothers, bringing joy and laughter to the entire group with their playful antics. The elder whales would often indulge the calves, engaging in playful games and teaching them the vital skills needed to thrive in the ocean.

Life in the group was full of happiness and friendship. They swam together in synchronized formations, moving as if following the ocean's rhythm. When the sun touched the horizon, painting the sky with bright colors, the group would gather to enjoy the warm evening light. As night fell, they shared stories under the stars, communicating with clicks and whistles, sharing their experiences with remarkable precision.

Rose, the wise matriarch, became a mesmerizing storyteller, captivating her audience with her rich and expressive narratives. Drawing from her own journey and the stories her mother, Eve, had shared, she inherited a wealth of wisdom and guidance from her ancestors.

Her stories painted a vivid picture of their oceanic world, opening the young ones' eyes to the wonders and mysteries beyond their watery home. She spoke of the vastness of the ocean, the endless stretches of blue that held countless secrets waiting to be unraveled.

Through her narratives, Rose conveyed the delicate balance that sustains life in the ocean, emphasizing respect for each other's spaces and roles within the ecosystem. Her stories warned of the dangers beyond the pod's safety, speaking of the mysterious shadows that lurked beneath, the predators that navigated the dark waters, and the risks of venturing too close to the surface where humans roamed.

Phil, the eager and impressionable calf, hung on to every word of his mother's tales, feeling an even more intimate connection to his mother and to the rich history of their species.

The pod's tales not only entertained the young ones but also served as vital lessons in survival and adaptation. Rose, the wise elder of the group, began to recount a few unforgettable experiences.

"Listen closely, little ones," Rose's voice resonated through the deep blue, her tone a mix of authority and warmth. "This happened before your time. The ocean bed erupted with lava, disrupting the entire marine world and causing chaos in the ocean." Rose was referring to a tsunami that occurred in the Pacific Ocean.

One young whale, wide-eyed with curiosity, asked, "What happened next, Rose?"

Rose's eyes darkened with the memory. "The strong waves tested our strength and resilience. All the adult whales formed a protective circle around the young ones to shield them from nature's fury. I was young then, and our matriarch was Eve. She was wise and strong. Eve instructed us to move away from the eruption, but the ocean's disruption broke our formation. Some young and even mature whales got lost."

The pod listened in rapt silence, the weight of the story pressing upon them. "Despite calling out, we couldn't locate all of them. Some reunited with us after a few days, but three—two young calves and one adult male—never returned. Above the ocean, human ships were being destroyed, and many human lives were lost at sea. Countless other marine creatures fled; many lost their lives. It was a tough experience for all of us."

The young whales huddled closer, their eyes wide with fear and awe. "What did you do when it was over?" another young whale asked.

Rose's gaze softened, filled with memories of calmer times. "We rested and rejoiced in our survival, but we also mourned the missing family members. We learned to cherish every moment, to stay united, and to always be prepared for nature's unpredictable fury."

The young whales nodded, the lesson sinking deep into their hearts. Rose's story was not just a tale of survival; it was a reminder of the strength of their bond and the importance of staying together, no matter what challenges the ocean might bring.

Let me tell you another story, a happier one. Once, we encountered a group of friendly dolphins." The youngest calf, eager for more, asked, "Dolphins? What were they like?"

Despite her usual stoic demeanor, a glimmer of amusement flickered in Rose's eye. "Those little dolphins," she reminisced, "were brimming with youthful energy. They darted around us, taunting us with their playful clicks and whistles, before finally issuing a challenge: a race. Being the larger creatures, we readily agreed, only to discover after a long and exhilarating stretch that their agility and bursts of speed far outmatched our own. We were simply no match for them. Not one to be deterred, we proposed a contest of a different nature – a dive to see who could descend the furthest. The dolphins, ever enthusiastic, readily accepted. With a powerful flick of our tail, we plunged into the depths, the water pressure increasing with each passing meter. It wasn't long before I saw the playful glint fade from their eyes as they struggled to keep pace. They soon gave up, surfacing with a mixture of disappointment and awe. The score, as they say, was tied." A chorus of excited voices filled the water. "What did the dolphins do then?" one calf asked.

"They laughed and congratulated us," Rose said. "It was a moment of joy and camaraderie. We found unity and joy in our shared celebration of life, showing that even in the vast ocean, we can find friends and allies."

The young whales marveled at the tales, absorbing the lessons of bravery, resilience, and friendship. Rose's stories became part of the pod's legacy, a testament to their shared experiences and the wisdom passed down through generations.

As the night wore on, the pod would rest together in peaceful slumber, their melodic calls fading into the tranquil rhythm of the ocean. Through Rose's storytelling, the young whales learned about their oceanic world and imbibed the essence of their tradition.

The storytelling sessions became a cherished tradition, a sacred bond that connected them to the past and the limitless possibilities of the future. Through the stories of the pod, they found solace, guidance, and a profound sense of belonging to something greater than themselves.

Chapter 3

The Orca's Hunt

For hunting, the pod consistently depended on Rose's guidance and strategy. On a particular day, they had identified an optimal location to hunt for squids, finding them in significant numbers. As the matriarch, Rose instructed all whales to dive deeper into the ocean's depths for food. Still a young and curious calf, Phil waited eagerly at the surface. His excitement grew with every passing moment, knowing that the pod's dive often led to exciting discoveries and new experiences.

Rose, the matriarch, and the other adult whales glided gracefully through the water as they descended to great depths. Their sleek bodies moved with precision and grace, a testament to their years of experience and mastery of the ocean's currents.

As they dove deeper, the ocean pressure increased, but the whales were well-adapted to these conditions. They had evolved over millennia to withstand the challenges of the deep, their bodies equipped with specialized adaptations to thrive in this mysterious world.

Phil watched in awe as the adult whales disappeared into the depths, their massive forms slowly fading from view. He knew that the ocean's depths held many wonders and dangers, and he could not wait to explore it all one day.

Meanwhile, unable to withstand the immense pressures of such depths, the young calves reluctantly gave up on their hunt and resurfaced for a breath of fresh air. As they rejoined Phil at the surface, their curious eyes scanned the horizon, anticipating their mothers' return.

Amidst the tranquility of the ocean, a haunting sound reached Phil's ears—the distinct and chilling calls of the Orca pod. Instantly, a shiver of fear ran through him, for he knew all too well the predatory nature of these menacing creatures. The orcas, also known as killer whales, were known to be cunning and ruthless hunters, and their presence filled the ocean with an air of tension and danger. This pod consisted of at least 30 Orcas.

Phil recognized the urgent need for help and called out to his mother and the other adult whales, hoping they would hear his plea. His heart raced with anxiety as he scanned the vast expanse of the ocean, searching for the familiar and reassuring sight of the protective pod forming a barrier around the vulnerable calves.

The orcas' call grew louder with each passing moment, signaling their approach. Phil asked all the other calves to huddle together, seeking comfort and safety in each other's presence. Phil and the other calves kept on calling the adult whales for their rescue.

Phil's call finally reached the adult whales, who immediately ceased their hunting and swiftly resurfaced, forming a protective barrier around the vulnerable calves. The orcas, known for their predatory nature, approached the pod with menacing intent. They aimed to separate the calves from their adults' protective formation, testing the adults' resilience and determination.

The orcas were cunning and strategic in their approach, trying to exploit any weaknesses in the pod's defense. They circled around, attempting to find an opening that would allow them to isolate one of the calves.

The haunting calls of the orcas grew louder, echoing through the ocean as they closed in on their prey. Phil's heart pounded with both fear and determination. He knew that the orcas were formidable adversaries, and the memory of their previous encounters haunted him.

But he also drew strength from the united front presented by the pod. The adult whales stood solid and resolute, ready to defend their young ones at all costs. Phil felt reassured, knowing he was not alone in this perilous situation.

The orcas, sensing the pod's defensive formation, hesitated momentarily. They were cunning and strategic hunters, known to test the resilience of their prey before making their move. They circled around the pod, assessing their targets and looking for any weaknesses in their defense.

Phil watched in awe and fear as the orcas circled closer, their dorsal fins breaking through the water's surface like dark shadows. He knew the orcas were experts at isolating and separating their prey from the pod's safety.

But the adult sperm whales were not easily fooled. They moved with purpose and precision, keeping a tight formation that left no room for the orcas to exploit. Each movement was coordinated, a dance of unity and strength that sent a clear message to the predators—they would not allow their young ones to be taken without a fight.

With her years of experience, Rose knew the orcas' tactics all too well. She remained vigilant, scanning the waters for any sign of danger. Sensing movement, she called out, her voice strong and commanding, "Everyone, do not break the formation! Ensure the calves are protected from all angles. The orcas will try to break our circle; don't let them."

A young whale, trembling with fear, asked, "Rose, what if they get too close?"

Rose replied, her tone firm but reassuring, "Trust in our strength and unity. Stay close to each other. We will protect you."

The tension in the water was palpable as the orcas approached, their sleek bodies slicing through the depths with predatory precision. Rose's heart pounded, but she remained calm, her years of wisdom guiding her every move. "Remember, we are stronger together," she reminded the pod.

As the orcas made their move, Rose and the other adult sperm whales responded with swift and coordinated action. "Hold the formation and scare them off with our loud clicks!" Rose commanded. The whales tightened their protective circle around the calves and began producing loud clicks.

The combined cacophony of loud clicks from the pod, including the young calves, disoriented the orcas and made them halt. The intense sound was irritating and forced them to reassess their attack strategy.

One orca darted forward, trying to slip through a gap, but Rose was ready. With a powerful flick of her tail and her loud click, she drove the intruder back. Another orca tried to flank them, but the adult whales moved as one, thwarting each attempt with precision. "They're testing us," Rose said, "but we won't let them win."

The young whales watched in awe as the adults skillfully blocked the orcas' every move. "They're incredible," one calf whispered, eyes wide with admiration.

The battle raged on; the orcas were relentless in their pursuit. But Rose and her pod held firm, their coordinated efforts a testament to their bond and strength. "We are stronger together," Rose repeated, her voice echoing through the water, instilling courage in the hearts of her family.

But despite their valiant efforts, the orcas' persistence paid off, and they succeeded in steering two calves away from the protective formation. It was Sam and Phil himself. Orcas tried to drown these isolated calves by not allowing them to breach the surface to breathe. All whales, including Sperm whales, are mammals and need to resurface to breathe.

Phil struggled desperately to resurface, his lungs burning for air, his heart pounding with fear and desperation. He called out to his mother, hoping she could hear him and come to his rescue. Hearing his cries, Rose broke through the barrier to rescue the calves. However, a couple of orcas attacked her, keeping her at bay. Even Rose's loud clicks could not break her free. Meanwhile, the other orcas were busy trying to drown Sam and Phil. Their cunning tactics proved a formidable challenge.

Desperation filled Rose's eyes as she struggled to save her son once again. She could not bear the thought of losing her calf to the merciless predators. Just as hope seemed to fade, a miracle unfolded before her eyes.

A male sperm whale, long and strong, appeared on the scene. It was Jack, a mature male sperm whale who preferred to swim alone. Determined and powerful, he bashed his massive head into the oncoming orcas, using his strong tail to strike at the remaining attackers. His loud click was enough to send shivers down the entire Orca pod.

Phil's heart pounded with fear and relief as he witnessed this incredible display of strength. Jack's intervention saved him from a grim fate, and he felt overwhelming gratitude and admiration for the brave and selfless male sperm whale.

However, the orcas were relentless. They shifted their focus to Sam, another calf. This time, the orcas employed a cunning tactic to keep Jack away from Sam. Backed by their pod's entire strength and coordinated precision, they managed to isolate Sam and keep him submerged underwater for prolonged periods. Despite Jack's desperate efforts, the orcas succeeded in their grim task.

Jack fought valiantly to save Sam, but his efforts were in vain. Sam's death was a painful reminder of the dangers lurking beneath the ocean's surface and the fragility of life. Jack engaged the orcas and led them in circles, creating a diversion that confused the predators and allowed the pod to escape. Finally, after an eternity, the orcas appeared to lose interest. They regrouped again and turned away, their haunting calls gradually fading into the distance, and started devouring Sam.

The pod remained vigilant, watching the horizon closely even after the orcas had disappeared. They knew the ocean was dangerous, and their journey was far from over. Grateful for Jack's protection and guidance, Phil and the other young whales swam back to the pod with a newfound appreciation for their father figure. A sense of relief washed over them as they reunited with their mothers and the rest of the pod.

As the tension subsided, Phil felt a mix of emotions. He was grateful for his family's protection and wisdom and felt a profound sense of belonging within the close-knit pod. However, they all mourned for the loss of one of their family members.

The orcas' hunt had been a stark reminder of the harsh realities of the ocean, where the delicate balance between life and death hung in the balance. But it had also reinforced the power of unity and love, for it was the collective strength of the pod that had thwarted the orcas' attack.

Chapter 4

An Unusual Bond

As the days passed, the bond between Phil, Rose, and Jack grew stronger, forming an unusual but profoundly affectionate family unit within the pod. Jack had come not just for procreation, but there was something more that drew him to Rose and her calf. Perhaps it was the sense of family and love that permeated the pod, or it was the spirit of adventure that seemed to thrive among them.

Rose's eyes twinkled with gratitude and affection as she introduced Jack to Phil. "This is Jack, your father," she said, her voice filled with pride and love. It was an unexpected and heartwarming revelation for Phil, who had grown up without knowing his father. He looked at Jack with curiosity and awe, realizing that this majestic male whale was his father.

Jack embraced Phil with warmth and love, his massive flippers wrapping around the young calf in a protective and nurturing embrace. There was an unspoken understanding between them, a connection that transcended the boundaries of the pod. Jack instinctively knew and cared for his son despite being absent during Phil's early years.

In the following days, Jack spent time with the pod, interacting with the other members and forming connections with the eligible young females. His presence brought a sense of harmony and protection to the group, and the females felt safe and comforted by his strong and wise demeanor.

Phil enjoyed his time with Jack, eagerly listening to the adventurous stories the older whale shared. Jack's tales were filled with awe-inspiring encounters with other marine creatures, his experiences spanning vast stretches of the ocean. Each story was a glimpse into a world of wonder that lay beyond the familiar waters of the pod's home.

Listening to Jack's stories, Phil felt a sense of wonder and excitement building within him. He yearned to explore the vast ocean, to witness the majestic creatures and hidden mysteries that Jack had encountered. But he knew that he was still young and not yet ready to face the dangers of the ocean on his own.

As he swam alongside Jack, learning from his wisdom and experiences, Phil made a silent promise to himself. He would wait patiently until he was old enough and strong enough to venture into the vast ocean, just like his father had done. He knew that the knowledge he gained from Jack would be invaluable when the time came for him to embark on his own adventures.

With each passing day, the bond between Phil and Jack deepened, and the pod witnessed a remarkable transformation within the young calf. He began to exhibit the same sense of wisdom and determination that Jack displayed, and he carried himself with a newfound confidence and strength.

Jack, in turn, took pride in his son's growth and development. He saw a reflection of himself in Phil, a legacy of resilience and courage passed down through generations. He knew Phil was destined for greatness and vowed to continue guiding and supporting him as he journeyed through life.

But amidst the joy and camaraderie, Jack's eyes showed a hint of sadness. He knew that his time with the pod was limited, as male sperm whales were known to be solitary creatures. He had come for a specific purpose; once that purpose was fulfilled, he would have to continue his solitary existence.

Jack's time with the pod ended as the days turned into weeks. He had fulfilled his role in procreation, and it was time for him to bid farewell to the group he had come to love. He shared a tender moment with Rose, expressing his gratitude for their love and connection.

He then turned to Phil, his son, his pride, and joy. "While you're with the pod, learn our ways, understand the dangers of the ocean, and most importantly, learn about humans. Remember, my son, your mother and the pod carry the wisdom of many generations," Jack said, his deep voice resonating with emotion. "The ocean is vast and unpredictable, but I know you will navigate it with grace and courage. Always trust yourself and your instincts, and never forget the love and guidance surrounding you. Anyway, I will be nearby, also heading south. I will meet other pods along the way and make new friends."

Tears welled up in Phil's eyes as he embraced his father one last time. He knew this was a bittersweet farewell that marked the end of an unusual but profound bond. Jack had become more than just a father; he had become a mentor, a protector, and a cherished friend.

Jack swam away from the pod with a heavy heart, his powerful form disappearing into the ocean's depths. Phil watched him go, a mixture of sadness and gratitude filling his heart. He knew he would carry his father's lessons and love with him, guiding him through every challenge and adventure that lay ahead.

As the days turned into months, Phil continued to grow and thrive within the pod. He embraced his role as a member of the close-knit family, forming strong connections with the other members, especially with his mother, Rose. Jack's absence was a constant ache in his heart, but he knew that his father's presence lived within him.

The ocean became his teacher, bringing new lessons and experiences every day. Phil navigated through the currents, learning the art of hunting, and honing his communication skills with the other whales. He ventured into uncharted territories, discovering the wonders and mysteries hidden beneath the waves.

But as he swam through the ocean, Phil never forgot the unusual bond he had shared with Jack. His father's words echoed in his mind, guiding him through moments of doubt and uncertainty. He drew strength from the love and sacrifice of his mother, Rose, and the wisdom and protection of his father, Jack.

Phil knew that his journey had only just begun. Countless adventures awaited him, and he was determined to face them all with the same courage and resilience his extraordinary family had instilled in him.

Chapter 5

Phil's Curiosity and Mother's Wisdom

As Phil grew older, his curiosity about the dangers around him intensified. One day, unable to contain his questions, he approached his mother, Rose, with excitement and anxiety. He wanted to know more about the dark threat of whaling, a subject that has been long avoided.

Rose sensed her son's eagerness to learn and his apprehension about the harsh realities of their oceanic world. She knew the knowledge she was about to impart would be heavy and distressing, but she also understood the importance of honesty and awareness in their fight for survival.

Rose asked Phil to talk a swim with her. With a deep breath, Rose began recounting her own harrowing encounter with whalers. Her voice trembled with emotion as she described the humans cruel and merciless practices.

"Phil, my dear," Rose began, her voice heavy with sorrow, "time and again, we have faced unimaginable dangers from humans. Humans would approach in large ships armed with sharp objects; These sharp objects are designed to pierce our thick blubber and muscle."

In one of my stories, I mentioned Eve, our former Matriarch. Except for the adult members of our pod, no one knows the full story of her death. She died sacrificing herself for the pod—a true testament to the role of a Matriarch. Eve was the bravest whale I have ever known, braver even than many adult male sperm whales.

I remember the day vividly, a day that tested our courage and resolve. The horizon was marred by the sinister silhouette of whaling ships, their harpoons glinting menacingly under the unforgiving sun. Panic surged through our ranks, but Eve remained unshaken. With unwavering determination, she made a fateful decision.

She positioned herself between us and the looming threat, her massive form a shield against the deadly harpoons. She knew the peril she faced, yet she advanced toward the ships with a resolve that left us awestruck. Her head-on confrontation with the whaling ships bought us the precious time we needed to escape. She rammed the vessel like a formidable force of nature.

In sacrificing herself, Eve embodied the essence of a true Matriarch—selfless, courageous, and unwavering.

Her legacy lives on in the hearts of those who witnessed her final act of valor, a poignant reminder of the sacrifices made for the safety and future of the pod.

Rose's eyes welled with tears. "Once Eve was too weak to fight, the humans dragged her lifeless body onto their ship. The once graceful and powerful tails would be used to pull us away from our ocean home, never to return."

Phil felt a surge of anger and sadness. "Why do they hate us so much? Do they hunt other marine life the same way, Mother?" he asked, his voice trembling.

Rose sighed deeply. "My dear Phil, humans have forgotten the sacred bond that connects all living beings. They see us and many others as mere resources to be exploited. Humans are driven by greed and their own desires, which are derived from our bodies. Their need blinds them to the pain they have caused and the balance they have disrupted."

Rose continued softly, "Every life is important, Phil. Just as we depend on Squid, Krill, and other creatures for survival, all species depend on one another. But humans kill us not just for food, but for greed, and that greed is not justified."

Phil, though young, began to grasp the profound connection his mother spoke of. "I understand, Mother."

Rose nodded, her eyes brimming with a mix of sorrow and pride. "Always remember that we must do everything we can to protect our home and each other," she said softly. "Almost every pod has lost someone to these whaling ships. Let's return to our pod, and keep this story to ourselves. I don't want to frighten the young calves."

Over time, Phil's curiosity grew, but so did his determination to protect his kind. He knew he needed to learn more about the world beyond their pod to understand their adversaries. He longed to explore the ocean's wonders and seek knowledge that could help him protect his family and their ocean home.

Seeing the fire in her son's eyes, Rose supported his thirst for knowledge. She knew the world was vast and full of wonders, and she encouraged him to explore it with an open heart and a wise mind.

Chapter 6

The Terrifying Encounter

On an unfortunate day, concern narrowed Rose's eyes as she observed two approaching mid-sized ships. She recognized them by the distinct markings on their hull. These were the same ships that, under the pretext of research, had left a trail of death and devastation in their wake, and she knew that the pod was in grave danger. Long ago, such vessels were also called Commercial Whaling ships, which hunted whales for their meat, blubber, and more.

Rose sounded the alarm without hesitation, alerting the entire pod to the imminent threat. The once tranquil atmosphere transformed into one of urgency and fear. The adult whales immediately formed a protective barrier around the vulnerable calves, strategically positioning themselves to shield them from potential harm. Phil's heart pounded in his chest as he swam closer to his mother, seeking the reassurance of her presence. He could feel the collective anxiety of the pod, and he knew that they needed to act quickly to ensure their survival. The two whaling ships represented a formidable adversary, armed with deadly harpoons and driven by a relentless pursuit of their kind. One among them was bigger but slower, and the other was smaller but faster.

As the whaling ships drew closer, the humans aboard seemed aware of the majestic beings in the water below. These ships are equipped with Passive sonar detectors, which listens for clicks produced by whales or any disturbance caused by their movement through water.

Rose's eyes never left the ship, her instincts guiding her to make the best decision for her family's safety. She had seen the devastation that whaling could bring, and she was determined not to let history repeat itself.

With a decisive movement, Rose urged the pod to act as one. "Everyone, stay close and follow me," she commanded, her voice steady but urgent. "We must move quickly."

The pod responded instantly, their synchronized retreat a testament to their unity. As they swam away from the approaching vessel, their massive bodies slapped against the water, creating a symphony of powerful, echoing waves.

"Mother, why are we running?" asked young Phil, his voice trembling with fear and confusion.

"Humans are coming, my son," Rose replied, her tone laced with urgency. "We must stay together and keep moving. They are dangerous."

"Rose, will we be safe?" another young whale asked, fear evident in their voice.

"We will be safe if we stay together," Rose reassured, "Trust in our strength and unity. We have faced numerous challenges previously and survived; we will survive this as well. We are a family, and we protect each other."

As the ships drew closer, the tension in the pod grew. "Tim, take the rear and ensure no one falls behind," Rose ordered. "We can't afford to lose anyone." Tim was the giant eight-year-old adult male whale.

"On it, Rose," Tim responded, positioning himself at the back of the group, his massive presence a shield against any potential threat.

The pod moved as one, their movements graceful and synchronized despite the urgency. The sound of their bodies slapping against the water echoed through the ocean, a powerful reminder of their strength and resilience.

"Keep pushing forward," Rose encouraged, her voice unwavering. "We are almost clear of the danger."

With every powerful stroke, the pod inched further away from the vessel. Their unity and determination were palpable, a testament to their bond and Rose's leadership.

The whaling ships, however, were relentless. They accurately tracked the pod's exact location with their Passive Sonar detectors. The ships soon caught up to the pod. For the pod, the whaling ship represented a dark threat they could not underestimate. Rose knew their clicks were ineffective against these ships, and the only chance of survival was to outswim them and put as much distance as possible between themselves and the relentless hunters.

As they swam with all their might, Phil could feel the rush coursing through his veins. He had never experienced anything like this before, and the fear and excitement intertwined within him. His mother's teachings echoed in his mind, reminding him of the dangers they faced and the importance of staying together as a united front.

The whaling ships persisted in their pursuit, their engines roaring as they closed the distance between them and the pod. The humans on board were determined to get as close as possible to kill the magnificent creatures.

Rose's heart pounded with each stroke of her powerful tail, leading the pod in a desperate escape. The ocean around them churned with intensity, reflecting the moment's urgency. But the whaling ships seemed relentless, their harpoons ready to strike at a moment's notice.

In the face of danger, the pods drew strength from each other. They communicated with powerful clicks, a testament to their unity and resilience. They were not just a group of individuals; they were a family, a community, and they would protect each other at all costs.

As the minutes turned into an hour, the ship's determination showed no signs of waning. Rose's leadership was unwavering, and her focus on leading her family to safety was clear and resolute. She was determined to keep the whaling ships from succeeding in their pursuit.

But despite their best efforts, the whaling ships continued their relentless chase. The humans aboard seemed unyielding in their quest.

Just when all hope seemed lost, a sudden and unexpected change in the ocean's currents offered a glimmer of hope. Like an unseen hand from the depths, a powerful current swept the pod in a different direction, propelling them away from the pursuing vessel.

Rose seized the opportunity and urged the pod to go against the current, swimming with all their might. They moved with a speed and grace that only desperation could summon, their massive bodies cutting through the water like torpedoes. The pod now had a good head start over the ships.

The whaling ships, caught off guard by the sudden change in direction, struggled to adjust their course. The pod had gained a momentary advantage, and they used it to put as much distance as possible between themselves and the ship. But the ocean was vast, and the whaling ships were persistent. They continued to pursue the pod.

Despite the odds stacked against them, the pod persevered, their unity and determination driving them forward. They knew their survival depended on staying one step ahead of the whaling ship, outsmarting their pursuers, and using the ocean's vastness to their advantage.

It appeared as though fate had thrown yet another lifeline to the pod. The struggle against the relentless ocean currents led to an unexpected engine malfunction in one of the ships, which abruptly and temporarily halted its pursuit. The other ship also suspended its pursuit. Exhausted and momentarily relieved, the pod slowed its pace. The pod had now managed to evade the whaling ships and had a good lead over them.

Chapter 7

Being Bait

The following day dawned upon the weary pod of whales, their massive bodies still feeling the lingering exhaustion from their daring escape. As they floated on the ocean's surface, their minds weighed heavy with the uncertainty of their situation. Rose, their wise matriarch, observed the restless waters keenly, ever vigilant to the dangers lurking beneath the waves.

Sensing her pod's unease, Rose knew they could not afford to linger in one place for too long. The relentless pursuit of the humans would not cease, and they needed to devise a plan to outmaneuver their hunters. With a sense of urgency burning in her heart, Rose gathered her pod around her, their massive forms creating a protective circle in the vast expanse of the ocean.

"My dear family," Rose began, her voice resonating with determination. "We cannot afford to remain idle while the threat of humans looms over us. We must act and continue swimming south toward the safety of our home to ensure our survival." Rose was referring to the Southern Oceans, a protected sanctuary for whales as declared by the International Whaling Commission in the mid-20th Century.

Southern Oceans are not only safe havens for whales but also provide their delicious food source, i.e., the squid and krill. These waters with abundant food supply would provide them with sustenance and shelter.

"We must move as one," Rose urged, her words carrying the weight of their collective destiny. "Together, we can overcome any obstacle that stands in our way. But we must act now before it is too late."

Despite Rose's urgency, the pod hesitated, their weary bodies reluctant to embark on another arduous journey. The journey was almost five days long. The memory of their harrowing escape was still fresh in their minds, and they feared the unknown dangers that lay ahead.

But Rose would not be deterred. With unwavering resolve, she implored her pod to trust in her leadership and believe in the strength of their bond as a family. "We have faced adversity before, and we have emerged victorious," she reminded them. Together, we are unstoppable."

By the time Rose could have influenced the pod, misfortune struck once more. The relentless whaling ship caught up to them, and the previously malfunctioned vessel was nowhere in sight. Only one ship, the larger of the two, continued its relentless pursuit.

Chaos erupted within the pod. Rose, understanding the calculated strategy of the humans, knew they aimed to exhaust the entire group and then target individual whales. Given the pod's already fatigued state, this tactic threatened to succeed. She decided to act as bait and give the pod a chance to escape. Without hesitation, Rose took charge, urgently summoning the attention of every member.

"Everyone, listen!" Rose called out; her voice filled with urgency. "We have to swim south at maximum speed, now!"

The whaling ship's captain realized the route taken by the pod and maneuvered to block their path south, forcing them north. As the pod route got blocked, they panicked and almost changed their direction. Rose quickly understood their strategy.

"Mary, make the pod dive deep and cross the ship," Rose commanded, turning to the next senior matriarch, "Phil, follow Mary and don't trail behind. Do not worry about me. I will join you soon. For now, let me lead the ship away from you all."

Rose's eyes met Phil's. "Stay safe, my son," she whispered. Then, louder, "Mary, dive deep and head south. Don't stop until you're clear of them."

Phil's heart sank as he heard his mother's words. He did not want to leave her side, but he knew her sacrifice was their only chance of survival. With tears in his eyes, he nodded at her and tried to convey his love and gratitude with a gentle nudge.

Rose smiled weakly at her son, her eyes shimmering with tears of sorrow and pride. "You are strong, my dear Phil," she whispered. "You have the spirit of a leader within you. I believe in you. Now carry on, and never forget the love we share."

With teary eyes, Phil swam away from his mother, the rest of the pod following Mary's lead. Rose watched them go, a mix of emotions swirling within her. She knew this might be the last time she saw her family, but she also knew she had to buy them precious time.

Under Mary's lead, the pod dove deep and swam south, leaving the ship behind. Meanwhile, Rose deliberately slowed her speed and swam north boldly and selflessly, making herself an easy target to divert attention and protect the rest of the pod.

The ship hesitated, caught off guard by the maneuver. Rose positioned herself near the ship, ensuring the humans would take the bait. The tactic worked; the ship began to follow Rose, who was deliberately swimming slowly.

"Come on, you monsters," Rose muttered to herself, swimming steadily, drawing the ship further away from her family.

Phil, watching from a distance, felt his heart ache with fear and pride. "Be safe, Mother," he whispered, following Mary as instructed.

Rose swam with all her might, her muscles burning, her heart pounding. She knew she had to buy the pod enough time to escape. As the ship closed in, she glanced back, seeing the determination in the humans' eyes.

"You won't get them or me," Rose vowed, her voice a mixture of defiance and desperation.

The chase continued, Rose's strength waning but her resolve unbroken. She could see the pod in the distance, disappearing into the depths, heading south. Relief washed over her; her plan was working.

"Just a little longer," she urged herself, pushing through the pain.

Realizing the pod had slipped away, the whaling ship turned its full attention to Rose. Her stamina ran out, but she kept swimming, every stroke a testament to her love and sacrifice for her family. As the ship drew closer, Rose felt a strange calm. She had done what she needed to do. She had given her pod a chance.

Rose's strength waned further, and her movements became slower and more labored. With one last surge of energy, Rose executed a daring maneuver, quietly diving deep into the ocean to evade the ship's pursuit. The crew on board struggled to follow her movements, unsure of her location in the vast expanse of the sea.

In the depths of the ocean, Rose's heart pounded with both fear and determination. Rose knew she could not stay submerged for long and needed to resurface eventually to breathe.

As Rose resurfaced to catch her breath, she spotted the research ship trailing behind, still searching for her. As soon as Rose surfaced for breathing, the ship's sonar picked her up, and the pursuit began. Rose attempted similar maneuvers repeatedly and soon realized that she was able to lose the ship if she dove silently. Rose now believed that she had a chance to survive.

As and when the whaling ship closed in on Rose, the crew prepared to shoot her with harpoons. But every time Rose dove deep and evaded. After an hour of pursuit, Rose could not dive anymore. The ship was now on top of her with harpoons aimed. As fate would have it, a miracle happened, a pod of dolphins, drawn by the commotion, swam toward the ship, creating their own diversion.

"Hey Rose, how are you doing? Are you still up for a race against us?" one of the dolphins said in a playful tone.

Rose, her voice tinged with exhaustion, replied, "I'd love to, but as you can see, my fins are a bit occupied today."

The matriarch of the dolphin pod swam closer, her eyes filled with concern. "Let us help you," she offered. "We'll create a distraction. You focus on escaping back to your pod."

Rose nodded gratefully, "Thank you. I owe you one."

"Don't worry about it," the dolphin matriarch replied. "Now, get ready. We'll draw their attention away. Swim fast and stay safe."

The dolphins danced and leaped in the water, distracting the crew's attention. The ship's crew found it difficult to accurately locate and aim at Rose.

The crew, now frustrated, had already lost the pod, and didn't want to lose this giant, magnificent whale as well. They readied their harpoons, aiming at the entire lot. Though dolphins were of no interest to them, they were about to become collateral damage. Multiple harpoons were shot. One of them hit a Dolphin, and it proved fatal. Another one grazed Rose's massive body. While the injury was not fatal, it made her bleed slightly. The trail of blood now made it easier for the hunters to track her.

On the other hand, Phil was torn between his love for his mother and his survival instincts. He hesitated momentarily, torn between wanting to protect his mother and obeying her plea to escape. But in his heart, he knew what he had to do. Once the pod had reached a safe spot where the whaling ships were not visible, he told Mary that he was going back to check on his mother.

With profound affection for him, Mary advised Phil against returning. Rose had entrusted his well-being to Mary, but Phil's thoughts were solely occupied by his concern for Rose. Ignoring Mary's counsel, Phil swam back toward his mother, unable to bear the idea of leaving her behind in such a vulnerable state. Driven by his determination to remain by her side, he swam swiftly and caught up to his mom. His remarkable speed allowed him to quickly outpace the ship and reach Rose. When he arrived, he saw injured Rose.

Phil's arrival caught the attention of the humans, who now saw him as an additional easy target. As he reached Rose, he positioned his massive body protectively around her as if to shield her from further harm.

Rose was fighting dual emotions; on one side, she was unhappy that Phil was in danger too, and on the other hand, she was overwhelmed with love and pride for her son's bravery. She could feel his heart beating against hers, and in that moment, she knew that she had raised a whale of exceptional courage and compassion. The presence of Phil gave her tired and bleeding body more vigor to fight for both of them. They swam for a few hours, covering miles in the vast ocean.

Rose was tired and at her limit. The whaling ship also closed in on them; the whalers started preparing their harpoons again for the attack. Rose's heart pounded with fear for her son, but she had faith in his ability to escape. She watched as Phil was able to keep up with her comfortably. The whaler's primary focus was still Rose, recognizing her as the big prize.

Chapter 8

The Pursuit Continues

The whaling ship was equipped with advanced technology, and the crew had honed their skills in hunting whales. Harpoons were thrown at Phil and Rose, but they miraculously escaped initially. Rose knew it was only a matter of time before their luck ran out and one would be struck.

With a mix of fear and determination, Rose called out to Phil, her voice filled with urgency. "Don't look back, my dear Phil," she urged. "Keep going, keep swimming. I'll do what I can to protect you."

With a firm and resolute voice, Phil replied, 'Not this time, Mother. You need to listen to my plan. Let's swim in a random, unpredictable manner. That way, they won't be able to target us easily."

Rose's heart swelled with pride at Phil's bravery. "You're so strong, my boy," she said, her voice breaking with emotion. "Alright, let's do this together."

Phil swam closer, his massive form moving in perfect sync with Rose's. "We'll outsmart them, Mother. Just like you taught me."

The humans struggled to keep up as they began their unpredictable swim, creating a mesmerizing pattern in the water. Rose and Phil moved as one, their powerful bodies cutting through the waves with grace and precision. The bond between them was unbreakable, and in that moment, they were unstoppable.

"Keep it up, Mother," Phil encouraged. "We're confusing them. They're unable to aim accurately." Phil's eyes sparkled with determination. "We can do this, Mother. We'll get through this."

Rose smiled, feeling a surge of hope. "I believe in you, Phil." Together, they continued their dance in the ocean, their movements a testament to their unyielding spirit and love for one another.

While they swam hard, Rose was getting tired. She was at her peak, and her speed slowed down. The ship caught up to Rose with already ready harpoons, and they fired at her. One of the harpoons struck her dorsal fin, but it did not penetrate deeply; with a forceful push from her body, Rose managed to break free. Thankfully, the harpoon did not explode upon impact. Nevertheless, the wound was substantial, causing her to bleed profusely even more. Despite the excruciating pain, she adamantly refused to yield.

The humans started targeting Rose with another harpoon. Just as it seemed that the next harpoon would find its mark, the Passive Sonar detector picked up another huge object heading towards them. A large shadow appeared from the ocean's depths. It was Jack, Phil's father, who had been swimming nearby.

Jack surged toward the whaling ship, leveraging his colossal size and strength to collide head-on with the vessel. Despite its substantial size, the abrupt impact of the massive whale momentarily disrupted the ship's functioning. Now, the humans had to be wary of Jack, fearing that repeated collisions might damage the ship's hull and lead to its sinking. Jack's intervention provided Phil and Rose with a brief moment of respite.

Jack's colossal frame leaned in to examine Rose's injury. In a faint voice, Rose murmured, "Jack, I don't know if I can go on. You must protect Phil; he shouldn't be here today. Take care of our son!" Phil remained unaware of their exchange; his eyes locked on the approaching ship.

"Go, Phil! Swim away, find safety!" Jack's voice boomed over the waves. "Rose and I will keep them at bay and join you soon." With unwavering determination, Jack continued his valiant assault, ramming his massive head into the ship from every angle. Tears streamed down Phil's face as he watched his father bravely challenge the whaling vessel. He realized Jack was putting himself in harm's way to shield them, just as Rose had done earlier.

In his frustration, Jack shouted at Phil to heed his warning, threatening that he would be next to face his wrath. Phil understood the urgency and swam on, trailing the rest of the pod. As Phil swam, he couldn't help but glance back at his father, now locked in a fierce battle with the whaling ship. Jack's massive tail struck the ship, causing it to rock and sway dangerously as he skillfully avoided their deadly harpoons. Both Jack and Rose realized that this was the moment to sink the halted ship to prevent any further massacre of their species.

Rose knew that she had to join the fight. With a burst of energy, she swam back toward the whaling ship, using her powerful head and body to smash into the ship alongside Jack. The ship's hull was getting severely damaged.

But the whalers were not giving up either, and they continued to throw harpoons at Jack and Rose, hoping to weaken and capture them both. Jack fought back with all his might, but the odds were against him.

The crew of the whaling ship was now faced with a formidable challenge—two mighty sperm whales fighting to protect themselves and their family. They knew capturing such majestic creatures would bring them fortune and fame, but they also knew it would come at a significant cost.

Despite their fear, the whalers were determined to capture Jack and Rose. They had come too far to give up now and were driven by the desire for recognition and profit. Jack and Rose understood the best way is to avoid the front of the ship where harpoons are placed. With each strike of their powerful tails, they sent a clear message to the whalers—that they would not be taken without a fight.

Despite their bravery and strength, the odds were still against them. The whaling ship was equipped with powerful weapons and technology. The ship was revived again, and the relentless pursuit resumed. Jack realized that they could not keep fighting indefinitely. They were exhausted, and the whalers showed no signs of giving up. They needed a plan to outsmart their pursuers and find safety.

Jack instructed Rose to dive and resurface after swimming several miles south without making any sound, with Rose following Jack's trail. Despite feeling weak from blood loss, Rose agreed to the plan, and they both dove deep, swimming south in silence to avoid detection by the ship's sonar.

Throughout the dive, Jack constantly watched his tail, ensuring Rose's well-being. After covering a few miles, Jack felt confident that they were now safe.

However, when he looked back, he noticed Rose trailing far behind. Concerned, Jack stopped, returned to her, and gently nudged her head, encouraging her not to give up.

Aware of her limits and the dangers surrounding them, Rose spoke weakly, expressing gratitude for their excellent life and regret that she could not witness Phil's maturation. Despite her desire to spend more time with the pod, Phil, and Jack, Rose acknowledged her inability to swim further due to her weakened state. She implored Jack to care for Phil, transforming him into a resilient sperm whale capable of facing the world's challenges.

Realizing there was nothing more he could do, Jack witnessed Rose surface to take her final breaths. She gazed at the clear sky and vast ocean one last time, letting out a mournful cry that echoed across the sea—a farewell to her family and Phil. Heartbroken, Jack watched as Rose passed away.

Having picked up on their trail, the whaling ship arrived at the scene. The crew observed Rose's lifeless body and prepared to claim their prize by dragging her on board and mutilating her magnificent form. However, a group of large sharks, attracted by the blood trail, arrived at the scene as well. They were soon joined by orcas, which disrupted the crew's plans. The presence of Orca whales made the shark flee the scene. The orca whales now in significant numbers, took their time assessing the situation.

Before the crew could act, the orcas seized Rose's body and dove beneath the waves. The crew refrained from targeting the orcas. It seemed a fitting end for this magnificent creature. Nature intervened, preventing the beautiful creature from becoming a victim of human greed and allowing her to rest in her rightful place within the harmony of nature. The vow made by Rose came true: neither her pod nor herself were killed by the humans today.

It was a significant loss for the whaling ship. They decided to call it a day, probably out of fuel and with the crew also tired. Such loss is hard for them, but they often make up for such days with an even bigger catch from similar pods of whales.

Jack managed to escape the scene unharmed and circled back to the pod. Phil had already made it safely to the pod. Jack faced the difficult task of delivering the tragic news to the entire pod, including Phil, who was shattered by the loss of his mother. Overwhelmed with grief, Phil directed his anger toward Jack, blaming him for not protecting Rose.

The pod experienced profound sorrow; they had lost their matriarch, protector, and guide. Left to navigate the dangers of the ocean without her, they now had to confront the perils and challenges that lay ahead without the leadership they had relied on for so long.

In the days that followed, the pod mourned Rose's death. They swam in somber silence, their hearts heavy with grief. Phil, in particular, felt the weight of her absence. He had lost his mother, his mentor, and his best friend.

But during their grief, the pod found solace in one another. They came together, supporting and comforting each other in their time of need. They knew that they had to carry on, to honor Rose's memory by staying strong and united.

As days transformed into weeks, Mary took up the new role within the pod, becoming their protector and guide through the ocean's challenges. Having gleaned wisdom from Rose, it was Mary's responsibility to pass on those lessons to the rest of the pod.

With unwavering support and guidance from everyone, Mary embraced her leadership role. Leading the pod on their journey, she navigated the expansive ocean, confronting the perils that crossed their path. Recalling Rose's teachings—emphasizing the significance of family, the value of love and sacrifice, and the need to protect all living beings, regardless of differences—Mary steered the pod toward growth.

Encountering wonders and dangers as they swam, the pod faced them united in love and determination. Their journey was not solely their own; it was a chapter in the grand story of the ocean—a realm of wonder, beauty, and endless possibilities. Within this narrative, they were interconnected by a love without bounds, one that would carry them through whatever challenges the ocean presented.

After a couple of weeks, the pod arrived in the Southern Ocean, marking the end of their migration. They will spend a month here on their feeding grounds.

Chapter 9

A Father's Guidance

Jack remained with the pod for a month, observing how they gradually healed from Rose's death. Phil was also warming up to Jack. When Jack was confident that Phil had regained composure and was back on track, Jack decided to part ways from the pod and continue his solitary journey.

Expressing his wishes to the pod, Jack's departure was met with mixed reactions. Phil, who had just started reforming a connection with Jack, disliked the idea of him leaving, as Jack had provided strength and confidence to face potential dangers. Mary, however, was confident that the pod had regained the resilience to survive without Jack.

Phil expressed his interest in joining Jack on his adventures. Initially, Jack was not enthusiastic about the idea. However, honoring his promise to Rose to look after Phil, Jack eventually agrees to Phil's proposal and decides to take him along on the journey. This was a significant deviation from the usual behavior of an adult male sperm whale, who typically prefers solitude.

On the day of departure, Phil expressed heartfelt gratitude for the support the pod had given him and Rose throughout the years. He extended his well-wishes to all of them, expressing hope for frequent reunions. Mary embraced him warmly, providing the comfort he would expect from his mother, and wished him good luck on his adventures. She assured him the pod would always be his family, welcoming him with open arms whenever he chose to return.

As Phil swam alongside his father, Jack, he could not help but feel a mix of emotions. He was grateful for Jack's presence and guidance but also carried the weight of recent events. The encounter with the whaling ship and the loss of his mother, Rose, had left scars on his young heart.

Jack sensed Phil's inner turmoil and understood this journey was more than meeting new pods. It was a journey of healing, growth, and self-discovery. He knew Phil needed time and space to face his experiences and find his path in the vast ocean.

Jack decided to train him quickly on the whale's migratory paths and different types of clicks used by sperm whales in different situations. Whale migrations are often seasonal, with adult males migrating to colder waters during the summer and returning to warmer waters during the winter to breed. Jack was taking Phil to the Indian Ocean near Mauritius.

The weeks turned into months as Jack and Phil swam together, exploring new territories and encountering different pods of sperm whales. Jack introduced Phil to other whales, and while Phil was respectful and cordial, he could not help but feel like an outsider among them.

Jack notices Phil's reservations and has a heart-to-heart conversation with his son. They swam away from the rest of the pod, where they could talk in privacy.

"Phil, my son," Jack began, his deep voice carrying warmth and understanding. "I know that the recent events have been tough on you. Losing your mother was a devastating experience, and it's only natural to feel a sense of loss and uncertainty."

Phil looked at his father, his eyes filled with sadness and gratitude. "I miss her, Dad," he said softly. "I miss her guidance and her love. She was everything to me."

"I understand, Phil," Jack replied. "Your mother was a remarkable whale, and she loved you deeply. Her legacy lives on in you, and you carry her wisdom and love wherever you go."

"But I feel like I don't belong anywhere," Phil confessed. "I don't feel like I fit in with any pods. They have their own dynamics and relationships, and I don't feel a part of them."

Jack nodded thoughtfully. "It's okay to feel that way," he said. "Finding your place in the world is a journey and not always easy. But remember, you are not alone. You have me."

Phil looked at his father, his heart touched by Jack's words. "You're right, Dad," he said. "I am grateful for you and this journey we are on together. I want to learn from you and become a strong and wise whale like you."

Jack smiled, a sense of pride evident in his expression. "You already are a strong and wise whale, Phil," he said. "You showed incredible courage during the encounter with the whaling ship. Your mother would be proud of the young whale you have become."

As the days went by, Phil continued to learn from Jack. They practiced hunting techniques, explored ocean regions, and encountered marine creatures. Jack shared his knowledge and experiences, passing down the wisdom of generations to his son.

One day, as they swam near the surface, they spotted a playful group of dolphins leaping and splashing in the waves. Phil watched them with curiosity and amusement, feeling a sense of camaraderie with these lively creatures.

Jack notices Phil's fascination and decides to have some fun. He taught Phil how to ride the waves and leap out of the water like the dolphins. Phil embraced the challenge, and together, they joined the playful dolphins in their joyful dance.

At that moment, Phil felt a sense of freedom and joy that he had not experienced since the loss of his mother. The weight of his worries lifted, and he felt a renewed sense of purpose in the vast expanse of the ocean.

As the days turned into months, Phil and Jack encountered other marine species, each with its unique way of life. They swam alongside majestic humpback whales during their migration, and they observed the grace and beauty of sea turtles as they glided through the currents.

Through these experiences, Phil began to understand the delicate balance of the ocean ecosystem. He learned that every creature, no matter how big or small, played a crucial role in maintaining the harmony of their underwater world.

Phil's connection to the ocean deepened, and he realized that the sea was not just his home but a sanctuary, a place of wonder and magic that needed protection and preservation.

One day, as they swam near a coral reef, Phil noticed a group of humans snorkeling above. He remembered the encounter with the whaling ship and felt a surge of anxiety. But Jack reassured him, "These humans are not like the ones we encountered before. They are here to appreciate the beauty of the ocean and its inhabitants."

With Jack's reassurance, Phil cautiously swam closer to observe the humans. He watched as they marveled at the colorful fish and delicate coral, capturing the wonders of the underwater world with their cameras. Some of them even helped marine lives in distress, removing fishing hooks and, in some cases, nets wrapped around various marine life. Trusting one of these humans, Phil allowed them to get close. The human helped remove a rope stuck around one of his flippers.

As he observed the humans, Phil felt a glimmer of hope. Perhaps not all humans were like the ones who hunted his kind. Some could be allies and advocates for protecting the ocean and its inhabitants.

In the following weeks, Phil and Jack encountered more humans, some on ships conducting actual research and conservation efforts. They observed scientists studying whale behavior, collecting data to better understand and protect these magnificent creatures.

Through these encounters, Phil learned that people were fighting for the survival of whales and other marine species. He saw how passionate some humans were about preserving the delicate balance of the ocean ecosystem.

Jack emphasized the importance of these alliances, explaining that protecting the ocean required collaboration between whales and humans. "We are all connected," Jack said. "The survival of the ocean depends on our mutual respect and cooperation."

Phil felt a growing sense of purpose and determination as he continued his journey with Jack. He wanted to be a voice for the ocean, to advocate for its protection and preservation.

Their adventure was a journey of discovery, growth, and purpose as they swam side by side, father and son, two whales navigating the vast blue expanse, united by their love for the ocean and commitment to protect its wonders. Together, they would face whatever challenges came their way, knowing that they were not alone and carried the legacy of their pod, their family, with them wherever they went.

Chapter 10

A Remarkable Transformation

As a year passed, Phil grew into a magnificent and powerful sperm whale, embodying the best qualities of his parents, Rose and Jack. His father's guidance and care had a profound impact on Phil, shaping him into a wise and resilient individual.

Under Jack's watchful eye, Phil honed his hunting skills, mastering the art of finding squid and prey in the ocean's depths. He grew stronger with each passing day. As they celebrated their successful rescue, Phil could not help but feel a sense of pride and accomplishment. Phil had developed a keen sense of empathy for other marine creatures. He understood that every life in the ocean was valuable and that they all played a vital role in maintaining the ecosystem's delicate balance.

One day, as they were exploring the vast Pacific Ocean, they encountered a pod of sperm whales in distress. The pod's matriarch was isolated from the pod and targeted by whaling ships. However, this time, some brave humans who called themselves "Sea shepherds" were fighting against these whaling ships.

"Jack, get the pod to safety; I'll handle this," Phil urged urgently. Concerned, Jack asked, "But what about you?" Phil reassured him, "I'll be fine. I won't let another Rose fall today." With determination, Phil followed the matriarch, facing the whaling ships' danger. Though the ships appeared small, they posed a significant threat. As the Sea Shepherds intervened by attacking the Whaling ships with water cannons, Phil seized the opportunity to showcase his speed and strength. He toppled the two small-sized whaling ships with a powerful surge, creating panic and allowing the pod to escape to safety."

Soon after the incident, Phil accompanied Jack and the pod for some time. The entire pod looked up to Phil. Phil decided to stay with this pod for a while. He fathered a young female calf from a young female sperm whale. She was called Rose. Phil's journey had come full circle. From a young and curious calf to a wise and compassionate pod member, he had grown into a remarkable sperm whale.

Word of Phil's heroic act spread, reaching the ears of humans who cared deeply for marine conservation. The incident inspired many to act and be more mindful of their actions and impact on the ocean. But Phil's influence extended beyond the ocean's depths. Phil's story was shared through books, documentaries, and even movies, bringing his journey to worldwide audiences. People found inspiration in the tale of this magnificent creature who defied all odds and decided to fight for what was right.

Marine researchers studied Phil's behavior, seeking to understand the complexities of whale society and the bonds that formed between individuals. His story shed light on whales' intelligence and emotional capacity, challenging preconceived notions about their place in the natural world.

Phil's legacy also spurred advancements in marine conservation. Governments and international organizations took note of the public's response to his story and stepped-up efforts to protect sperm whales and enforce stricter regulations on whaling and other harmful practices.

Over time, Phil had accumulated numerous scars on his body, each telling a story of his battles and triumphs. These scars became his signature and were recognized worldwide. As Phil's fame spread, he became an icon for marine enthusiasts and animal lovers everywhere. People journeyed from distant places just to catch a glimpse of the legendary sperm whale and his pod, eager to experience the ocean's wonder through his remarkable story.

Through it all, Phil remained humble and faithful to his values. He always retained sight of the ocean's beauty. He knew that his journey was not just about him but about all the creatures of the sea and the delicate balance that sustained life in its depths.

Phil continued his journey alone without Jack. He led and helped many pods along the way. He always carried with him the memory of his mother, Rose, and her selfless sacrifice. He felt her presence in every moment, a guiding light that reminded him of the importance of protecting all life in the ocean.

And so, as the sun set over the shimmering Pacific Ocean, Phil's legacy lived on—a testament to the resilience of life, the transformative power of compassion, and the boundless potential that lies within every individual to shape a world that cherishes and protects the wonders of the natural world. The ocean, teeming with life and mystery, beckoned to all who would listen, offering a timeless invitation to explore its depths and embrace its endless possibilities.

Beyond the Story

Facts and Figures

For centuries, sperm whales were heavily hunted for their oil, spermaceti (a waxy substance used in candles and lubricants), and teeth (used for scrimshaw carvings). This intensive exploitation continued for centuries, reaching its peak in the 19th Century with the development of more efficient whaling technologies.

Estimates suggest that the global sperm whale population may have been as high as 1.1 million individuals before Commercial Whaling began. However, by the mid-20th Century, this number had plummeted by over 90%, with some estimates suggesting a decline to as few as 30,000 individuals. The sperm whale is listed as "Vulnerable" on the International Union for Conservation of Nature (IUCN) Red List due to past whaling impacts, ongoing threats, and the potential risk of future whaling. According to the International Whaling Commission (IWC), the estimated global population is around 600,000.

In 1985, the International Whaling Commission (IWC) implemented a global ban on Commercial Whaling for sperm whales. While this ban has played a crucial role in population recovery, sperm whales face threats. However, some countries, like Japan and Norway, continue Commercial Whaling activities, challenging the international ban.

Population recovery for sperm whales is slow due to their long lifespans and low reproductive rates. While some estimates suggest a gradual increase in recent years, the global population remains well below historical levels.

Beyond the international ban on Commercial Whaling, continued collaboration between nations and dedicated conservation efforts are essential for the long-term survival of sperm whales. These efforts encompass several key areas: developing and deploying technologies to minimize accidental entanglement in fishing gear, protecting critical marine habitats, reducing pollution levels in the oceans, and raising public awareness about the importance of conserving sperm whales and their role in healthy aquatic ecosystems.

Story 3

Even Death Cannot Separate Us

Chapter 1

The Serenity of Dairy Meadows

Once upon a time, in the idyllic countryside's heart lay Dairy Meadows, a picturesque dairy farm in Texas, USA, that seemed to have been plucked straight from the pages of a storybook. The mere sight of it was enough to transport anyone into a world of serenity and magic. Nestled among rolling hills and lush pastures, the farm was a sanctuary where time seemed to slow down, allowing the beauty of nature to reveal itself in all its splendor.

Anyone who sets foot on Dairy Meadows will instantly be captivated by its tranquil attraction. The air was infused with the sweet scent of nature, a harmonious symphony of blooming flowers and fresh grass that danced playfully with every gentle breeze. Cows roamed freely, their velvety noses grazing on the abundant green grass, embodying a sense of liberty that was rare and precious.

At the heart of this enchanting haven stood its owner and caretaker, Mr. Jamie. A man with a vast heart as vast as the meadows, he exuded kindness and compassion in every aspect of his being, or so it seemed.

It was home to a small yet joyful herd of around 300 cows, each with a unique personality and story. Among them was Daisy, a four-and-a-half-year-old Jersey cow who commanded respect from her fellow bovines with her gentle, firm, and nurturing demeanor. Her wisdom seemed to transcend her years, and it was no wonder that she often guided and comforted the younger cows when they needed assurance.

Daisy was a beacon of tranquility at Dairy Meadows. Her days were filled with a sense of contentment and fulfillment that radiated from her very being. She found joy in the simple pleasures of life at the farm, cherishing each sunrise that painted the sky with hues of pink and orange.

As the sun went down, Dairy Meadows glowed in golden light. Daisy, a cow, loved these peaceful evenings on the farm. During sunset, the world looked like it was dipped in gold. It was so calm and beautiful, making Daisy feel peaceful and happy. It showed how nature could be lovely and bring joy in simple moments.

The farm thrived under Mr. Jamie's watchful eye, and one could feel the deep bond of trust and understanding between him and the cows. He prioritized each cow's well-being, and in return, the cows reciprocated with a love and loyalty that was heartwarming to witness.

In moments of uncertainty or doubt, Daisy was the pillar of strength for her fellow cows. With wisdom beyond her years, she would gently guide and comfort the younger ones, offering them the assurance they needed to face life's challenges. In these instances, one would realize how much more there was to learn from these simple yet magnificent creatures that walk the same Earth as us.

In the embrace of Dairy Meadows, time seemed to lose its relevance. The days were filled with serenity and joy, and the nights were adorned with a starlit sky that whispered stories of wonder and dreams. The farm was more than just a place—it was a state of mind, a way of life that celebrated the beauty of nature and the profound connections that bound all living creatures together.

Chapter 2

New Arrival

As the seasons painted their vibrant strokes across the landscape of Dairy Meadows, the bond between Daisy and Mr. Jamie blossomed like the wildflowers in the meadows. With each passing day, their connection deepened, and it was as if they had developed a language of their own—a silent understanding that traversed the boundaries of human and bovine worlds.

Mr. Jamie's rough, weathered hands would gently stroke Daisy's ears, and in response, she would emit a soft, contented moo that resonated with a profound sense of peace. It was a language that transcended words—a language of touch and emotion that bound them together in a way only they could comprehend.

Daisy became Mr. Jamie's confidante and comforter in moments of joy and sorrow. The weight of the farm's responsibilities could sometimes become overwhelming, but as he sought refuge in Daisy's calming presence, it was as if the burdens were lifted from his shoulders. Her presence brought him a sense of tranquility and perspective, reminding him of the simple joys that life on the farm offered.

With their deep, soulful gaze, Daisy's eyes seemed to hold the universe's wisdom. As Mr. Jamie poured out his heart, she listened intently, her silent presence a balm to his weary spirit. It was as if she understood his worries without the need for words, and in those moments, a profound connection blossomed between man and cow.

The relationship between Mr. Jamie and Daisy was a testament to the beauty of inter-species friendships—a bond proving that love, understanding, and compassion could transcend the barriers of language and physical form barriers.

The herd thrived under Daisy's guidance, and unity and harmony pervaded Dairy Meadows. Each cow knew they were part of a more prominent family, and this sense of belonging fostered an environment of trust and security.

Daisy's relationship with Mr. Jamie deepened and evolved as the years passed. Their friendship became a source of strength and inspiration for both.

As the spring sun embraced Dairy Meadows, the air was filled with the sweet scent of blooming flowers and the promise of new beginnings. It was a season of hope and renewal, and at the heart of it all, the cows eagerly anticipated the arrival of new calves.

Stripped of natural romance, the cows undergo artificial insemination, with robust bull sperm carefully selected for the process. Unlike their counterparts in the wild, they lack the freedom to choose their mates or decide when to mate. However, having never experienced the intimate dance of mating firsthand, perhaps they do not yearn for it.

Among the expectant cows was Daisy, a gentle, nurturing soul who intuitively understood life's miracles. She had sensed the changes within her, the subtle shifts in her body that hinted at the presence of a new life growing inside her womb. As the days passed, her anticipation grew, and she embraced the weight of responsibility that came with being a mother.

Finally, the much-awaited day arrived—the day Daisy would welcome her calf into the world. As the first rays of dawn painted the sky with hues of pink and orange, Daisy's contractions began, signaling the imminent arrival of her little one. Amidst the beauty of the unfolding sunrise, Daisy's labor was a testament to the wonder of life and the raw strength of motherhood.

With each push, Daisy's heart swelled with love and determination. She could feel the bond with her unborn calf deepening as she brought him closer to the world outside. And then, in sheer magic, the little bull calf emerged, taking his first breath, and opening his eyes to the wonders around him.

Daisy nuzzled her newborn with a heart full of love, gently cleaning him with her tongue and showering him with the warmth only a mother's touch could provide. In that tender moment, Daisy knew she had given life to a beautiful soul, and from the depths of her being, she whispered, "Welcome to the world, my dear Jolly."

Jolly's energy was infectious from the very beginning. His spirited nature and playful antics brought joy and laughter to the entire herd. He would frolic through the meadows, his tiny hooves dancing on the soft grass, and the other cows could not help but watch with delight, their eyes filled with affection for the little calf who had stolen their hearts.

Under Daisy's watchful eye, Jolly grew stronger with each passing day. Her nurturing nature guided him as he learned to walk on his wobbly legs, and her gentle nudges encouraged him to explore the world around him. Jolly's confidence soared under his mother's loving guidance, and he fearlessly embraced every adventure that came his way.

Daisy took pride in her calf's exuberance and joy. To her, Jolly was not just another member of the herd; he was her precious creation, and she cherished every moment spent watching him grow and flourish. Their bond was woven with threads of love and trust, and it was evident to everyone at Dairy Meadows that Daisy and Jolly shared a connection that went beyond mere biology.

The other cows in the herd were enamored by Jolly's vivacious spirit. They often gathered around him, forming a protective circle, and showered him with gentle affection. It was as if they knew he was unique to Daisy and all of them.

Daisy had instilled a sense of community among the cows, and this camaraderie extended to Jolly. They became his guardians and playmates, and he, in turn, brought out the childlike innocence in each of them. The farm was filled with the laughter of the cows as they engaged in playful games and joyful gallops through the meadows.

As Jolly's character blossomed, so did his bond with Mr. Jamie, the guardian and caretaker of Dairy Meadows. He saw in Jolly the same adventurous spirit and resilience that he had witnessed in Daisy all those years ago.

Jolly learned the intricacies of life on the farm by observing everyone, including Mr. Jamie. The young calf followed him around, observing every move Mr. Jamie performed. From the art of plowing the fields to the gentle tending of the crops, Jolly soaked in the wisdom of his human companion with a sense of awe and admiration.

As Jolly grew, so did his love for exploration. He often wandered off independently, his curious eyes taking in the world's wonders. Daisy watched from a distance, her heart filled with pride and concern. She knew that her calf needed to explore, to discover his place in the vast mosaic of existence, but she could not help but worry about the dangers that lurked beyond the familiar boundaries of Dairy Meadows.

As days passed into weeks, Jolly grew into a healthy calf, embodying his mother's spirit. He carried with him the lessons of love and resilience that he had learned at Dairy Meadows, and he became a symbol of hope and inspiration to all who encountered him.

Chapter 3

A Heartfelt Separation

Early one morning, while Jolly frolicked with the other playful calves, a small truck made its way into the farm, driven by Jamie himself. Two farm assistants disembarked from the vehicle, swiftly lifting, and placing Jolly and other young calves at the truck's rear. These tender creatures were barely two months old, and from the back of the truck, they called out in distress, their plaintive cries echoing across the farm. The herd, sensing their distress, rushed to the scene. This separation was not an unfamiliar occurrence; it had happened before, but it was always heart-wrenching, especially for the new mothers among them.

Daisy and the other recent mothers darted around the truck, desperately trying to reach their calves. At one point, Daisy even positioned herself in front of the truck, a poignant testament to the depth of a mother's love. The anguished cries of the calves mirrored the pain in the cows' eyes as they followed the truck's slow exit from the farm and into another enclosure.

Daisy and her companions, positioned at the edge of the farm, watched and waited, their hearts heavy with hope that their precious offspring would soon be returned to them.

However, their hopeful anticipation gradually turned to despair as time ticked by. Jamie called out to the adult cows, urging them to return to their enclosure, yet the heavy weight of uncertainty hung over them. Reluctantly, the new mother cows complied, their hearts burdened with the absence of their beloved calves. Days turned into a week, and still, there was no sign of their young ones.

With each passing day, Daisy and Jolly adjusted to their new reality, where they can't even glimpse each other from a distance, deprived of the warmth of physical closeness. Daisy's maternal instincts pulled at her heartstrings, urging her to be close to her calf, to shield and care for him. She struggled to comprehend the significance and reasoning behind Mr. Jamie's decision.

After a week, Mr. Jamie noticed Jolly's health deteriorating due to being cut off from Daisy's milk. Jolly was reluctant to take the milk alternatives, which were crucial for his growth. These alternatives are specially formulated commercial products designed to mimic the nutritional composition of cow's milk, typically containing a blend of milk proteins, fats, and other essential nutrients. They come in liquid or powder form and are often mixed with water before feeding to calves.

Calves are separated from their mothers at an early age to prevent them from consuming all of their mother's milk, which would prevent farmers from being able to sell cow's milk commercially to humans.

Their connection remained unyielding, and they could communicate through gentle calls. Each evening, as the sun began its descent, Mr. Jamie would find Daisy standing by the fence, and sometimes, he would sit beside her, understanding the depth of her emotions. He would softly stroke her velvety ears, offering silent comfort and gratitude for the sacrifices she had made for the farm and its inhabitants.

Chapter 4

Little Lily's Arrival

The young master has a beautiful wife whom he had married 4 years ago. Their wedding was a celebration that echoed through the hills, with friends, family, and the animals of Dairy Meadows coming together to honor the union. The vows were exchanged under the open sky, resonating with the couple's hearts and the essence of the land they stood upon.

The couple had a three-year-old daughter called Lily. She connected the dots between past and present, bridging the cow's gentle soul and the child's innocent curiosity.

Daisy watched with tenderness and longing as she was cradled in her mother's arms. Seeing Lily being lovingly fed and cared for stirred emotions within Daisy, evoking memories of her days nurturing her beloved Jolly. It was as if fate had woven an intricate thread between their lives, drawing parallels between their roles as caregivers and nurturers.

The young master and his wife often brought little Lily to visit the cows in the lush pastures. It was a scene of both novelty and familiarity – a young Lily exploring the world with wide eyes and a mature cow Daisy gazing upon her with a mixture of affection and a touch of nostalgia. In their own quiet way, the cows seemed to recognize the connection as well, as if they understood the significance of the love that bound them together.

In the tender moments between the young master's daughter and the cows, Daisy found solace. The child's innocent laughter and reaching out over the fence to touch the cows' velvety noses were as if a circle of love was being completed. The legacy of care and compassion nurtured at Dairy Meadows was passed on to the next generation, an unbroken chain of understanding and empathy.

Yet, amidst the joy this new life brought to Dairy Meadows, there was also a bittersweet undercurrent. Daisy wondered how Jolly was faring, whether he was growing strong and joyful, just like the exuberant Lily she saw before her.

As the days passed, the bond between Daisy and the young master's daughter, Lily, grew more assertive. The little girl's cherubic face and bright eyes filled Daisy with joy and nostalgia. Daisy could not help but feel a special connection to the tiny human.

Little Lily's visits to the pasture became regular occurrences. She would giggle with delight each time as she watched the cows graze and play. Daisy, the cow, would stand by the fence, gazing back at the human Daisy with affection and longing.

The young master's wife noticed the cow's fondness for their daughter and often encouraged the interaction. She believed this bond between the two Daisys was magical, a connection transcending species and language.

As the days turned into weeks, Daisy the cow found comfort in being near Lily. The little girl's innocent laughter and playful spirit brought joy to the cow and the farm. It was as if Lily had a way of brightening even the cloudiest days, just like the sun that illuminated Dairy Meadows.

One evening, as the sun dipped below the horizon, the young master and his wife brought little Lily to visit the cows. The atmosphere was serene until the young master got a call that quickly escalated into a heated argument, drawing his wife into the fray. Their focus shifted from Lily, who, fueled by curiosity, wandered closer to the fence. This time, there was no one to stop her.

As Lily ventured inside the fence, the entire herd encircled her, their large bodies sniffing and licking her. At first, Lily found it amusing, but soon, fear gripped her, and she began to cry out for her mother. Jamie's wife, alerted by Lily's cries, rushed back to her rescue. However, before she could reach Lily, an aggressive cow approached, sniffed Lily, and struck her with its horn, sending her flying several meters away, unconscious.

As the cow prepared for another attack, Daisy stepped forward, warning the aggressive cow to stay back. The cow hesitated, then retreated, allowing Daisy to protect Lily from harm.

The entire incident unfolded before Jamie's wife's eyes as she raced to Lily's side. Lily eventually regained consciousness, fortunate to have escaped severe injury. Angered by the aggressive cow's actions, Jamie decided to isolate it from the herd. Soon after, it was loaded onto a vehicle and driven away from the farm, never to return.

Jamie and his wife had a newfound love for Daisy. They could sense Daisy's affection for their daughter, and they believed that their connection was a testament to the love and care Mr. Jamie and Lily had bestowed upon all the farm animals.

Every time Lily visited the herd's fence, Daisy would gently nudge her, and the little girl reached out her tiny hand to touch the cow's velvety nose. It was a tender moment that touched the hearts of all who witnessed it. The young master and his wife smiled, realizing that this interaction was more than a coincidence—a reminder of life's interconnectedness.

In the meantime, Mr. Jamie continued to care for the isolated calves, including Jolly, with unwavering dedication. The young bull had grown into a strong and confident member of the herd, and Mr. Jamie took pride in his role in his development. The bond between the cow and the caretaker remained unbreakable.

As Lily grew, she began to visit Dairy Meadows more often. She had learned to walk steadily, and now she could run through the fields and her laughter ringing through the air. Daisy would watch with adoration, her heart swelling with affection for the little girl.

One day, as Lily approached the fence, Daisy did something unexpected. She let out a soft moo, a sound filled with love and longing. The young girl looked up, her eyes meeting Daisy's, and she smiled. Lily imitated Daisy and let out her own moo. It was as if the two were having a silent conversation, a communication that transcended words.

From that day on, whenever Lily visited Dairy Meadows, she would respond to Daisy with her own moo. No matter where Daisy was on the farm, she would come running to her. It became a game between them, a secret language only they understood. The other cows watched with curiosity, marveling at the unique bond that had formed between the little girl and the cow.

One day, as little Lily approached her father, she held something. It was a drawing she had made, a beautiful portrait of Daisy and Jolly together under the shade of the ancient oak tree. The image captured the essence of their bond, the love and trust that transcended time and distance.

Tears welled up in Mr. Jamie's eyes as he saw the drawing. He understood the longing Lily felt to see Daisy and Jolly together, and he was touched by her empathy and compassion for the cow and her calf.

Chapter 5

Daisy and Jolly Reunited

As the cows grazed peacefully in the lush pasture on a fine morning, excitement and anticipation hung in the air. The isolated calves were moved to the adjacent enclosures. Among the gathering of curious young calves, Daisy's keen senses detected a familiar presence, and her heart skipped a beat with joy.

In this adjacent enclosure, Jolly, now a year old young and robust bull, also sensed something special. His ears perked up, and he turned his head toward the source of the melodic voice that called out to him. Daisy's gentle moo crossed the distance, reaching her beloved calf's ears like a long-lost melody.

Jolly hesitated momentarily, his bright eyes searching for the origin of the familiar voice. He had grown and changed since the days when he and Daisy were separated, but the connection they shared remained imprinted on his heart. With an eager heart, he followed the sound, his steps filled with curiosity and anticipation.

As Jolly drew closer, the scent of the meadows and the warmth of the morning sun enveloped him. He felt an inexplicable pull, as if an invisible thread was guiding him toward a profound moment in his life. As he approached the fence separating him from the other cows, he saw her – Daisy, his mother.

Time seemed to stand still as Daisy and Jolly locked eyes, their gazes filled with love, longing, and a profound sense of connection. Emotion overwhelmed Daisy, and tears of happiness rose in her expressive eyes. The moment she had been waiting for, she could now see Jolly. However, a fence was still separating them. Daisy was content with even seeing her Jolly.

With a joyful moo, Jolly leaped and pranced in excitement; the happiness in looking at each other was radiating through their every movement. Jolly was able to touch his mother's face with his face. He felt the warmth of Daisy's presence, the softness of her velvety nose against his own, and the assurance of a bond that could not be broken. Daisy, too, showered her calf with motherly affection, nuzzling him tenderly as if to reassure herself that this was indeed a reality, not a dream.

As the other cows in the herd watched the heartwarming scene, a sense of collective joy spread through Dairy Meadows. It was a testament to the enduring power of love and the unbreakable bond between a mother and her child. In the evening, Jolly and the other calves returned to their enclosures.

The following days were filled with pure happiness for Daisy and Jolly. Calves were allowed to meet their mothers from a safe distance, but they were separated to avoid milk dependency on their mothers. This method also ensured the mothers would be less depressed as they could see their calves and thereby produce more milk for the farmers.

Chapter 6

Silent Onset

Daisy beamed with pride as she watched her son enthusiastically embrace life. She was content knowing that Jolly was happy, healthy, and safe. Her maternal instincts guided her every step, and she took her role as a mother seriously, ensuring Jolly had the emotional support needed to thrive.

The presence of Jolly reduced the stress on Daisy, thereby increasing her milk production. Mr. Jamie was, in fact, taking advantage of this arrangement.

At the heart of Dairy Meadows, Mr. Jamie's dedication to the well-being of the cows remained unwavering. He knew the importance of a balanced diet and proper care, ensuring that each cow received the nutrients needed to stay healthy and produce high-quality milk. He made it a point to spend time with each cow, observing their behavior and ensuring they were content and comfortable. This care came at a heavy cost to Mr. Jamie.

Sometimes, a good diet alone is not sufficient to produce the desired amount of milk. To address this, Mr. Jamie would occasionally administer newly available bovine somatotropin (bST) injections to increase the cows' milk production. This drug was still in trial phases and not FDA-approved, making it cheaply available. Many dairy farmers resort to such measures to maintain profitability, turning it into a necessity for some. Mr. Jamie approached the task with care and gentleness, always prioritizing the well-being of his herd.

However, using non-approved drugs carries inherent risks. Daisy was the first to exhibit abnormal symptoms. Her once full and vibrant udders now felt different, a strange discomfort seeping through them. Despite her attempts to shake off the unease, the sensation persisted, causing her to lay softly in distress. Daisy knew she had to communicate her feelings to Mr. Jamie and hoped he would understand her plea for help. That night, she continuously cried out in distress.

Some of her herd members gathered around her to console her. Despite their efforts, there was no relief from the constant pain she was enduring. Daisy's cries across the farm woke Mr. Jamie from his deep sleep. He noticed the cries belonged to Daisy, sensed her agitation, and knew something was amiss. Without wasting time, he called for the farm's trusted veterinarian to examine Daisy. The vet arrived promptly, and his experience was evident in his approach to the situation, which was a mix of care and professionalism.

As Daisy stood calmly before the veterinarian, Mr. Jamie's watchful eye never left her. He knew how much she meant to the farm, and the thought of her suffering weighed heavily on his heart. The veterinarian conducted a thorough examination.

After a few days, the veterinarian approached Mr. Jamie with Daisy's results. They spoke in hushed tones, discussing the findings and potential implications. It seems Daisy was suffering from Mastitis, a persistent and potentially fatal mammary gland infection that leads to high somatic cell counts and loss of production. Mastitis is recognized by reddening and swelling of the infected quarter of the udder and whitish clots or pus in the milk. The cause of this ailment was attributed to the drug given by Mr. Jamie. On discovering this, Mr. Jamie promptly ceased using the drug on his cattle.

Daisy observed them from a distance, unable to comprehend their words, but the gravity of the situation was palpable. She sensed something was seriously wrong, and her heart ached for the comfort and reassurance only her master could provide.

Gathering his emotions, Mr. Jamie approached Daisy, his face a mixture of worry and tenderness. He cradled her gently, kissing her forehead to convey his love and support. Daisy felt the warmth of his touch, and even though she did not fully understand the extent of her condition, she trusted her master and the veterinarian. She knew they were doing their best to help her.

The following day, Daisy found herself isolated from the rest of the herd. The once-familiar faces of her fellow cows were replaced by a sense of solitude and uncertainty. Despite feeling lonely and separated, Daisy believed her master had a reason for this decision. She trusted that he was working diligently to find a way to make her well again.

As days turned into weeks, Daisy's isolation continued. Mr. Jamie visited her regularly, bringing fresh hay and water, but her condition prevented her from joining the other cows in the pastures. The separation from her herd and Jolly was taking a toll on her mental health. Like humans and many other animals, even domesticated animals long for companionship. Often, humans fail to understand that companionship can cure many illnesses, but greed blinds them to this simple truth.

The veterinarian also visited regularly, administering treatments, and carefully monitoring Daisy's progress. Though she did not fully understand the purpose of these treatments, she cooperated, trusting that her master and the vet knew what was best for her. The other cows in the herd, too, seemed to sense Daisy's situation, and they often gathered near the fence, offering their support through gentle moos and nods.

Mr. Jamie remained constantly in Daisy's life throughout this challenging time. As spring gave way to summer, Daisy's condition started to show little signs of improvement. She was unable to generate milk during this ordeal. The recovery was slow and steady, but the positive changes they observed encouraged Mr. Jamie and the veterinarian.

With each passing day, Daisy's resilience and spirit became more apparent. She had faced an uncertain and challenging period in her life, but through it all, she never lost faith in her master's care and the support of the herd. One afternoon, as the Dairy Meadows sunbathed in golden light, Mr. Jamie approached Daisy's enclosure with hope and anticipation. He had seen her progress and was cautiously optimistic about her recovery. He decided that it was time to reintroduce Daisy to the herd. The other cows sensed something important was about to happen and gathered near the fence, their curious eyes fixed on the scene unfolding before them.

As Mr. Jamie gently opened the gate to Daisy's enclosure, she looked up at him with eyes that seemed to mirror his hope and love. Slowly, she stepped out into the pasture, surrounded by the welcoming presence of her herd. The other cows offered her gentle nudges and affectionate moos, celebrating her return to their midst.

Daisy's resilience and the support of the herd had overcome the challenges she faced, and Mr. Jamie knew that this reunion was a testament to the strength of their bond. From that day forward, Daisy resumed her role as a guiding presence in the herd. She shared her wisdom and experiences with the younger cows, offering gentle guidance and support. Lily was also thrilled to have Daisy reintroduced to the herd.

As the seasons turned, Daisy had recovered but was still unable to produce any milk. She did not care much about it and relished every moment in the picturesque pastures of Dairy Meadows. However, it was turning out to be a financial burden on Mr. Jamie to look after such sick cows, which meant feeding them on time, ensuring proper shelter, and regular checks from the vet. Mr. Jamie had to take a tough call. It was the same year when the nation experienced an economic downturn, which resulted in reduced consumer demand for dairy products both domestically and internationally.

Suddenly, the ease from financial debt took precedence over the bond that had formed between Mr. Jamie, Lily, and Daisy. The trust built over the years was on the verge of being shattered.

Chapter 7

A Fateful Journey

One fine morning, the meadows were abuzz with an unusual flurry of activity. The cows sensed something was amiss, and a feeling of apprehension spread through the herd like a ripple in a pond.

Daisy's heart felt heavy as she watched some of her sisters, one by one, being led forcibly away from the pasture. They were pulled by ropes and loaded in a big hauler. Their worried eyes mirrored the same fear she felt. Each departure filled her with a sense of helplessness. But all she could do was offer silent prayers for their safety. She hoped that whatever awaited them was not as unsettling as it seemed.

Daisy had learned to trust Mr. Jamie. She tried to calm her nerves with a deep breath, knowing that her master always had their best interests at heart.

As the sun dipped below the horizon, casting a warm orange glow over Dairy Meadows, the tranquil atmosphere was disrupted by the arrival of the same men who had taken the other cows. Daisy observed them cautiously, their presence stirring a sense of fear within her. They carried ropes and seemed to be executing a plan, but she could not comprehend the reason for their visit.

However, her anxiety eased when she spotted her beloved master, Mr. Jamie, and Lily walking alongside the men. Mr. Jamie, along with Lily, approached Daisy and kissed her on the head; his eyes were teary. A wave of reassurance washed over Daisy as she thought that they might be here to help her, just like the veterinarian. She cooperated without resistance as the men led her away, although uncertainty lingered in her heart. Daisy was boarded onto a big livestock hauler.

"Where are they taking Daisy?" Lily asked, her voice tinged with curiosity and worry.

Mr. Jamie sighed softly, trying to muster a reassuring smile. "She hasn't been feeling well, sweetheart. They're taking her to a place where she can get better."

Lily's eyes widened with hope. "When can I see her again?"

Mr. Jamie knelt down to Lily's level, meeting her innocent gaze. His heart ached as he forced the words, "Soon, my love. As soon as she's healed, you'll see her again."

As a twist of fate, some young calves, including Jolly, were also loaded into the hauler. Daisy was finally united with her calf. Unfortunately, she could only caress her calf and was in no condition to feed her.

Daisy and Jolly were now in the company of some known herd members and some unknown herds taken from other farms. As the hauler left Dairy Meadows, its engine's rumble filled her ears, making her wonder where this journey was leading. Despite not knowing the destination, she clung to the belief that her master had orchestrated this for her well-being, hoping that this path would cure her ailment, allowing her and Jolly to return to Dairy Meadows. Despite Jolly being in good health, why is he accompanying me? Does he have any problems that our master is aware of? These questions additionally tormented Daisy.

The journey stretched for several days, and Daisy was accompanied by her calf, Jolly. The presence of her precious offspring brought her both comfort and concern.

"Mom, where are we going?" Jolly asked, his voice trembling. Daisy nuzzled him gently, trying to mask her own fear. "Don't worry, Jolly. Everything will be fine. Just stay close to me."

"But I miss the meadows," Jolly whispered, his eyes wide with anxiety.

"I know, dear," Daisy replied softly. "Remember the stories I used to tell you? The meadows, the warmth of the sun, and the love from our master? Hold on to those memories. They'll keep us strong."

As the hauler rolled on through the dark of the night, Daisy continued to whisper tales of their serene home and the care they had once known, hoping to fill Jolly with the same sense of trust and belonging she held dear.

"Mom, will we ever see the meadows again?" Jolly asked, his voice a mere whisper.

Daisy sighed, her heart aching. "I don't know, Jolly. But no matter where we are, we'll always have each other. And that's something they can never take away from us."

She reassured him with gentle moos, promising that everything would be fine. As the vehicle rolled on in the dark of the night, Daisy would whisper stories, hoping to fill Jolly with the same sense of trust and belonging she held dear.

Finally, the vehicle stopped at a place that was both unfamiliar and yet strangely welcoming. The scent of fresh hay and the sound of contented cows filled the air. Daisy stepped out, accompanied by Jolly, and looked around curiously.

Daisy hesitated momentarily before stepping out, her hooves touching the foreign ground beneath her. The climate felt warmer and drier compared to the lush pastures of Dairy Meadows. The landscape was different, with unfamiliar trees and plants dotting the horizon. The cows around here were of various breeds, some appearing healthier, some sick, and many calves as young as Jolly. Daisy felt like a stranger in this new land, far away from the comforting familiarity of the meadows she had known all her life.

The uncertainty of her surroundings weighed heavily on Daisy's heart. She missed the rolling hills and soft green grass of Dairy Meadows and the scent of the sweet clover that had become a part of her daily life. The cows around her seemed content, but she could not help but feel anxious and alone in this strange environment.

Daisy stuck with Jolly because she could not identify other members of her herd. She promised him that they would return to their farm soon and that this situation was only temporary. But to her dismay, the unfamiliar men led Jolly and the other calves away, leaving her feeling even more isolated and vulnerable.

Among unknown cows and in an unfamiliar land, Daisy found it challenging to connect with them. Their language seemed different, and the ways of this new farm were foreign to her. She longed for the comforting presence of Mr. Jamie, who had always understood her needs and desires, but he was nowhere to be seen.

After two days, Daisy still struggled to adapt to her new reality. She missed the camaraderie of her fellow cows back at Dairy Meadows and the guidance she had offered to the younger members of her herd. Here, she felt like an outsider, disconnected from the rhythms and routines she had known for so long.

Yet, Daisy's resilience persisted. She remained determined to make the best of her situation. Drawing on her wisdom and experience, she sought to find common ground with the cows around her. Slowly but steadily, she forged connections with some of them, offering her gentle support whenever needed.

In this new land, Daisy encountered a kindred spirit in Bella, an older cow who had experienced a similar journey from her home farm. Bella understood Daisy's challenges and quickly became her companion during this transition. Bella had been on this farm for just two days longer than Daisy. The two cows spent hours reminiscing about their homes, finding solace in each other's company amidst the unfamiliar surroundings.

A glimmer of hope flickered within her heart as Daisy listened to Bella. The possibility of finding a permanent cure for her ailment gave her renewed strength and determination. She knew she had to believe in Bella's stories, that cows brought here from different places returned healed. It was a ray of hope shining through the uncertainty of her current situation.

Bella became Daisy's confidant during their time together in the new land. One day, Bella shared more stories from other cows she had met.

"Daisy," Bella began, her voice filled with conviction, "I've seen so many cows come and go. This place must be special. They enter that shed over there, and I've never seen them back on this farm. It has to be a healing place."

"You really think so, Bella?" Daisy asked, her voice trembling with hope. "What if we're just fooling ourselves?"

Bella shook her head. "No, Daisy. Trust me. I've been here a few days longer than you and seen the trucks. They probably take the healed cows back to their farms. I've not heard their painful moos as they leave. What else would they do with us cows in that shed?"

Daisy glanced at the shed Bella pointed out. "So, all those sick cows... they went in there and never came back here on the farm?"

"Exactly," Bella said, her eyes shining. "Our turn will come, Daisy. We just have to be patient a little longer."

Daisy took a deep breath, feeling a renewed sense of hope. "Alright, Bella. I'll believe in your stories. We'll get through this together."

As they watched the shed and the trucks outside, they couldn't help but dream of the day they would be healed and returned to their respective farms. The hope of a cure and the bond they shared gave them the strength to face their uncertain future with courage and determination.

Chapter 8

A Cruel End with a Twisted Consolation

After a few days, more cows lined up to enter the shed. Bella, Daisy, and Jolly were all included. However, there was a separate queue for grown cows and a separate one for calves.

Right from the shed's footstep, the atmosphere was unsettling. Daisy got an ominous feeling from this place. Machines hummed and clanged, filling the air with loud, jarring sounds that sent shivers down Daisy's spine. The cries of cows who had gone before her echoed all around, which further intensified her fear. Every instinct told her to resist, to run back to the safety of the pasture, but she could not muster the strength to fight and return to the rest of the herd.

With her heart pounding, Daisy steeled herself and was forced to step inside the shed with other cows. The unfamiliar surroundings and the sounds were overwhelming, but she reminded herself there must be a reason for all this. Mr. Jamie had always acted in their best interests, and she believed this was no different.

As the machines roared to life, Daisy's heart pounded so loudly it drowned out all other sounds. She watched in horror as other cows were placed into a small machine, where a manually operated bolt was struck in their forehead, rendering them motionless. Once dead, their bodies were hoisted upside down, and their throats were slit. Blood covered the entire floor.

This image portrayed a chilling testament to the cruelty of this place. Her eyes welled with tears as she witnessed the suffering of her fellow creatures, and she could not fathom why humans would subject another living being to such pain. Her mind was filled with questions and a profound sense of sadness. How could this be happening?

"Why, master? Why would Mr. Jamie, a person who cared for her and all his herd, allow this nightmare to befall her?" Daisy's thoughts raced with confusion and worry. She could not comprehend why she was going through this ordeal. Had she done something wrong to deserve such a fate? Was this a punishment for some unknown transgression?

Her thoughts soon raced back to Jolly, her precious calf. Amid this horrifying scene, she clung to the hope that he was safe and far away from this nightmarish place. She yearned to see him again, to reassure him of her love and that she would always be with him, even if they were physically apart. However, she could only see him, not reach him.

Despite the fear and uncertainty, Daisy resolved to stay strong for herself and Jolly. She knew she had to endure this ordeal to protect her calf and preserve the hope of reuniting with him. She vowed to survive, not just for herself but also for all the cows around her who were subjected to this unimaginable cruelty.

The calves were handled in a separate queue. Soon, it was Jolly's turn. Daisy yelled, "Stay strong, Jolly! Do not worry; we will meet again; this will end soon."

Jolly, pulled by a rope, cried out, "Mommy, where are you?" The calves were slaughtered the same way as adult cows. Jolly's cries echoed in the shed, calling out to Daisy for help.

Daisy couldn't bear Jolly's cries. She yelled, "I am here, my love; stay strong; it will all be over soon. Mommy is coming behind you. We will be together once this is all over."

Daisy thrashed her head, trying to free herself from the ropes. She managed to break loose and rushed towards Jolly, attempting to hit the men operating the machine with her horns.

"Help me, someone, please!" Daisy called out, but no one dared to revolt and defy their fate. More men were called into the shed to control Daisy. They brought in more restraints. Daisy mustered all the strength left in her, thrashing wildly. The men struggled to hold her down. Finally, she slipped on the floor, soaked in blood. The men seized the moment to shackle her hind legs, restricting her movements. Still, she fought on, driven by the desperate need to save her calf.

Unfortunately, the men continued their processing of the calves. They stunned Jolly in front of her in the machine. Once Jolly was motionless, he was strung upside down, and his throat was slit open in front of Daisy. Gust of blood started oozing out of him. The sight put immense shock on Daisy; she was weeping profusely. She wanted to go and hold him for one last moment to ease his final pain. She was trying harder to fight her restraints. The men were finding it difficult to contain her. At this moment, she wished she could be with her calf for one last time. Finally, they decided to shoot her using a Bolt Gun outside the confinements. With a loud thud sound, Daisy was motionless. She could not move or think. Her eyes were fixated on Jolly and in these final moments.

Without remorse or compassion, the men continued their grim task of processing the dead cattle for their meat. The mechanical hum of the processing machines filled the air, accompanied by the sharp clang of metal against metal.

Once the butchering was complete, the meat was meticulously packed into frozen containers and sealed tight to preserve its freshness. These containers would then be loaded onto trucks and shipped to various butcher shops or stocked in the meat counters of supermarkets across the region. It was a chilling realization that a loving cow who had served humans for its entire life would soon be reduced to mere commodities, packaged, and sold for human consumption.

Yet, amidst the grim reality of their situation, there was a strange and unsettling consolation. As the workers sorted through the meat, they placed Daisy and Jolly's heads together in a display at a nearby supermarket. It was a macabre scene, their lifeless eyes staring out from the confines of the meat section, a haunting testament to the cruelty of their fate.

In a twisted twist of fate, it seemed as though destiny sought to reunite them even in their tragic end. The sight of their severed heads on display served as a painful reminder of the callousness and indifference that still existed in the world. It was a stark contrast to the warmth and love they had once known on the farm, a reminder that even the strongest bonds could be severed in the face of human greed and exploitation.

Beyond the Story

Facts and Figures

As of 2021, the global cattle population was estimated to be around 1.5 billion individuals. Cows are the primary source of beef globally, with an estimated 70 million cattle slaughtered for meat annually in the United States alone.

Many cows raised for meat and dairy are kept in confined animal feeding operations, often involving crowded and unsanitary conditions. Cows may undergo painful procedures without adequate pain relief, such as dehorning and castration. The slaughter process can be stressful and cause suffering for cows despite regulations requiring humane handling.

It is important to note that farming practices vary significantly, and some farms prioritize the well-being of their animals. However, the abovementioned concerns represent significant challenges within the large-scale cattle farming industry.

Studies suggest cows are intelligent animals with good spatial memory, problem-solving skills, and the ability to learn and remember complex tasks. Research indicates cows can experience various emotions, including joy, fear, grief, and stress. They form strong social bonds with other cows and exhibit signs of mourning when separated from their calves. We have a moral obligation to treat these animals with respect.

Story 4

Gentle Giants

Chapter 1

Nature's Majesty

The intricate tapestry of life within the animal kingdom is woven with myriad tales of captivating creatures, each with unique behaviors and social structures. Among these, the majestic elephants stand out, awe-inspiring giants of the reserves and forests. Renowned for their imposing physical presence, they also boast a social structure that is as complex as it is fascinating. In this fourth chapter, we embark on a journey into the captivating world of the elephant herd, a testament to the marvels of nature's design.

Elephants exhibit a profound sense of camaraderie and cooperation that shapes their way of life. The herd, often comprised of several individuals, forms a community that transcends mere proximity. It is a bond forged through shared experiences, mutual dependencies, and an intricate web of communication that extends beyond human comprehension.

A typical elephant herd is a symphony of life orchestrated by various characters. At the helm of this harmonious ensemble stands the matriarch, a remarkable figure that carries with her the weight of age, wisdom, and experience. The matriarch, usually the group's eldest and most seasoned female, is a living library of survival strategies. Her long life has exposed her to the myriad challenges and triumphs of the wilderness, endowing her with invaluable knowledge that sustains the herd's existence.

Her role, however, extends far beyond being a living library of survival strategies. The matriarch is the guiding force, the compass that directs the herd's movements and decisions and shapes its very existence. When the herd is in search of water, navigating through dense undergrowth, encountering potential threats, or enduring harsh seasonal migratory journeys, her guidance illuminates the path. Her choices are influenced by a complex blend of instinct, memory, and an uncanny ability to perceive environmental cues imperceptible to most. Her role is pivotal, and the survival of the entire herd often hinges upon her judgment.

Yet, the matriarch does not bear this responsibility alone. Surrounding her are other remarkable females, forming a formidable sisterhood of protectors, nurturers, and teachers. These female elephants, akin to the matriarch in their depth of experience, contribute collectively to the fabric of the herd's existence. In a society where shared responsibilities strengthen bonds; they collectively care for the herd's young and vulnerable. Calves, those wondrous symbols of hope and renewal, are not just looked after by their biological mothers but by the entire community, a testament to the compassion and care that permeates the herd.

As we explore their world, we find ourselves drawn into the compelling story of the elephant herd—a story that transcends words and touches the deepest chords of our human understanding.

Chapter 2

The Mana Herd

Amidst the vast expanse of South Africa's untamed wilderness is a tale of a remarkable elephant herd known as the "Mana Herd," a name that resonated with the very essence of their existence. Here, in the heart of the African landscape, where life thrived in its rawest and most captivating form, the herd's saga unfolded—a story of unwavering resilience, kinship, and the enduring spirit that defined their journey.

The Mana Herd, often called the "Majestic Herd," commanded attention and respect, much like the mythical beings of old legends. With its long and storied history, this herd held a special place in the hearts of those who shared the land with them. They had endured famines, predation from Lions, and various diseases. Their presence was a testament to the unyielding spirit of life, a symbol of the intricate dance between survival and harmony.

At the heart of this harmonious symphony stood one figure, a matriarch whose name resounded through the collective memory of the herd—Grace. Grace was not merely a name; it reflected her character, an embodiment of the qualities that defined her role within the Mana Herd. Aged nearly Forty years, Grace stood as a paragon of experience and wisdom, her presence a beacon guiding the herd through the challenges the wild had to offer.

The composition of the Mana Herd was a portrait of diversity, a mosaic of interconnected lives that painted the landscape with their unique stories. Among the herd were three newborn calves, delicate yet robust symbols of the cycle of life. These young calves, their futures unwritten, added a touch of vulnerability and hope to the fabric of the herd's existence. One among them was Eleanor. Eleanor was Grace's youngest daughter. She was a year old. Grace's bond with Eleanor was a testament to the enduring ties that bound the herd together. This legacy transcended generations, a cycle of care and guidance that ensured the continuity of their lineage.

Some elephants had crossed the threshold of infancy and were in the bloom of youth—four elephants between the ages of four and six. Their exuberance echoed through the reserve, a testament to the vitality that infused the herd with its pulse.

The mature females were the pillars upon which the herd's foundation rested. After Grace, we had Susan, Grace's next in command and most caring elephant.

Then there were Naomi and Teresa, the other mature female Elephants. Their collective experience served as a reservoir of knowledge, ensuring the survival of future generations.

Nestled among them were two young bull elephants, their presence marking a juncture in their lives. Approaching the age of ten, they stood on the cusp of transformation. One of these bulls, Jerry, belonged to Grace. The time was coming when their paths would separate from the close-knit embrace of the herd, guiding them on solitary journeys to find their place in the broader fabric of elephant society. This transition from the herd's safety to the challenges of independence is crucial to the herd's dynamics. Grace also had a firstborn named Satao. He embarked on his journey when he reached twenty-two years of age.

In the herd's presence, one could sense the pulse of time itself—the heartbeat of countless generations before and the promise of those that would follow.

Chapter 3

Satao's Return

In the heart of the African wilderness, a new chapter in the saga of the Mana Herd was about to be written—one that would resonate through the reserve, a testament to the eternal cycles of life, love, and survival.

Satao, once a young and spirited calf, had undergone a remarkable transformation within the embrace of the Mana Herd. Time had shaped him into a powerful and formidable bull elephant, his magnificence reflected in the curvature of his tusks and the authority with which he traversed the land. His journey from a curious calf to a majestic bull was a testament to the experiences that had molded him into the embodiment of strength and Grace.

With the approaching mating season, Satao felt the ancient call reverberating through his veins. The intensified musth stage in all the matured male bulls in the neighboring vicinity signaled the presence of females in estrus. This primal call stirred his instincts, summoning him to participate in the timeless ritual of courtship and reproduction. The winds carried with them the scent of anticipation, an invisible thread that connected Satao to his roots and beckoned him back to the fold of the Mana Herd.

His return wasn't merely coming home; it marked a crucial moment, a juncture where the past merged with the present, and destiny revealed its complex web. The Mana Herd awaited his arrival, their collective consciousness attuned to the rhythms of the wild, sensing the imminent shift in dynamics that his presence would bring.

Satao's arrival was nothing short of awe-inspiring. His physicality commanded attention—muscles rippled beneath his dark, weathered skin, and his tusks curved like ivory towers, a testament to his stature and dominance. He exuded an aura of authority, a presence that spoke of the trials he had overcome and the lessons he had learned.

Satao's journey back to the Mana herd was not without its trials. His path was marked by fierce battles with other bull elephants, each encounter a testament to his strength and resolve. One such struggle was with a formidable bull named Temba. Temba, a seasoned warrior, had tusks chipped from numerous fights, and his hide bore the scars of many confrontations. The clash between Satao and Temba was intense, their tusks locking in a contest of strength and willpower. The ground quaked under their weight as they pushed against each other, neither willing to yield. Ultimately, Satao's superior strength and strategic acumen prevailed, leaving Temba to retreat with a newfound respect for his opponent.

Another significant encounter was with a younger, yet equally ambitious bull named Kittu. Though less experienced than Satao or Temba, Kittu had a fire in his eyes and a drive to prove himself. Their battle was more of a test of agility and endurance than sheer strength. Kittu's speed and agility made him a challenging opponent, but Satao's experience and tactical mind prevailed. After a prolonged struggle, Satao outmaneuvered Kittu, demonstrating that wisdom often trumps youthful exuberance.

Both these battles lasted for over a day. These battles were more than mere displays of physical prowess. They were rites of passage, each stepping toward cementing Satao's place as a dominant bull. They were also reminders of the constant struggle for power and survival in the wild. Apart from these famous recorded battles, Satao faced numerous challenges he easily defeated. Despite his victories, Satao remained humble, aware that each battle could have gone differently. His scars were a testament to the resilience and perseverance required to thrive in such a competitive environment. On his journey, he met many herds and fathered many calves, spreading his lineage across South Africa.

Chapter 4

The Fierce Battle

Satao's journey had come full circle. From a young bull leaving the herd to establish his legacy to a dominant challenger returning to protect and guide his family, his story was one of resilience, strength, and enduring bonds. When Satao finally reached the Mana herd, his arrival was met with mixed reactions. The females were pleased to see him, their memories of his protective nature still fresh. The calves, curious and unafraid, approached him with wide eyes, sensing the strength and security he brought. However, the presence of other bulls in the vicinity, including Duke, created an undercurrent of tension.

Duke, the reigning dominant male bull of the region, was a force to be reckoned with. Around Thirty years old and in the prime of his life, Duke's authority had been unquestioned—a title earned through battles, displays of strength, and the recognition of his peers. Duke viewed Satao's return as a direct challenge to his authority. The ensuing struggle between Satao and Duke was inevitable. Unlike his previous encounters, this fight carried a more profound significance. It was about dominance and reclaiming his rightful place within the herd. The clash was going to be epic in scale, a titanic struggle that drew the attention of every creature within earshot.

The atmosphere was thick with tension as two adult bull elephants, both in their musth, faced off in this parched land. Their eyes locked, filled with the primal fury and determination that comes with this heightened state of aggression. Tusks clashed with a resounding crack, sending echoes across the landscape. Each elephant used its sheer mass and strength, pushing and shoving, trying to overpower the other.

Dust rose in clouds around them, mixing with the scent of sweat and musk. Their trunks coiled and whipped, aiming blows at each other's vulnerable spots. Ears flared wide, they trumpeted loudly, the sound reverberating like thunder. The ground beneath them trembled with each colossal impact, as they dug their feet in, determined not to yield an inch.

In this brutal battle, their foreheads collided repeatedly, the sound resembling distant gunfire. Bloodied and battered, neither seemed willing to back down. The stakes were high—dominance, territory, and mating rights were on the line. Their battle was a testament to their might and resilience, a raw display of nature's unyielding power.

The herds beyond the Mana Herd watched in curious silence. The battle for dominance was not just a spectacle; it was a glimpse into the intricate dynamics that defined the realm of the wild. The stakes were high, for the victor would claim the right to mate with the females and become a living embodiment of strength and survival.

Despite his experiences and victories, Satao found himself matched by Duke's raw power and determination. The battle was grueling, each elephant giving it's all in a contest that tested their limits. The herd's females watched with bated breath, their loyalty to Satao unwavering but their respect for Duke undeniable. As the fight raged on, it became clear that this battle would shape the herd's future, a future that relied on the outcome of this battle.

Neither was willing to yield. Their hefty trunks collided, and trumpets reverberated, warning all creatures to avoid the area. Day morphed into night as the two bulls invested their essence into the contest. They took occasional breaks to regain strength, remaining vigilant for the other's next move and avoiding surprises. Night surrendered to dawn, yet neither bull showed signs of retreat.

Amid the battle's tumult, Grace, the matriarch whose wisdom had guided the herd through numerous challenges, observed the spectacle with concern and understanding. As the struggle continued, she silently witnessed the ebb and flow of power.

During the height of musth, male bulls become unpredictable and may pose a threat to calves or any herd member. They struggle to distinguish between rivals and allies in the moment's intensity. Grace's concern grew, extending beyond the realm of power and conquest. The herd's welfare was paramount, and the safety of all calves and the other females weighed heavily on her heart. The thunderous clash of Satao and Duke had transformed the reserve into an arena of danger.

Grace communicated her decision to the other females with low rumbles and subtle gestures. It was time to leave, to seek refuge in a distant part of their territory. As the herd gathered around her, the atmosphere was one of purpose—a unity forged in the crucible of survival. The calves, innocent and unaware of the battle that raged, followed the lead of their mothers, their steps carrying the promise of a safer haven.

Grace led the charge, her presence a beacon that guided them through the changing landscape. As the distance between the battlefield and the departing herd grew, the reserve seemed to exhale as if releasing a collective breath it had been holding. The echoes of the battle slowly faded, leaving behind an aura of both tension and release—a reminder that life's struggles were often more intricate than they appeared on the surface. But amidst this tension, there was a glimmer of hope, a promise of a brighter future for the herd.

Graced hoped the battle would be resolved when they returned to their familiar territory, the dust settled, and the outcome decided. Her heartbeat was not only for the well-being of her herd but also for the victory of her beloved son, Satao—a victory that would carry within it the echoes of the past, the spirit of the present, and the promise of the future.

After hours of relentless combat, Duke was exhausted, struggling to remain on his feet. Satao, too, had nearly depleted his reserves of energy. Summoning every ounce of his remaining strength, Satao charged and rammed his head into Duke, sending him crashing to the ground. The tide of battle had clearly turned in Satao's favor as he repeatedly toppled the once-mighty Duke, asserting his dominance.

"Had enough?" Satao gasped, his voice breathless but still commanding.

While trying to get up, Duke glared at Satao with defiant eyes. "Know your place, child. I eat bulls like you for breakfast. Don't get ahead of yourself."

Satao had the upper hand for most of the fight, delivering blows that struck at Duke's pride. Time and again, he sent Duke crashing to the ground, chipping away at his ego.

"You don't have to be ashamed of this loss," Satao said, his tone almost sympathetic. "You had your time. Now it's the next generation's turn."

Duke's voice trembled with both fatigue and stubbornness. "I'm not done yet," he rumbled, refusing to concede defeat. This encounter was unlike any before; for Satao, victory would not come quickly.

Chapter 5

A Mother's Grief

The next day, as the sun painted the savanna gold, the herd finally returned home and to the battlefield, where their lives had changed forever. Grace, the wise leader who had guided them through countless challenges, walked in front, her steps heavy with worry and a mother's instinct.

But the sight that greeted her, unleashed a wave of grief, disbelief, and despair. Victorious, Duke stood triumphant among the shifting sand and memories of the past. Yet his victory was lost in the absence of another—a missing piece that tore through South Africa like a sharp knife. Satao was missing.

Grace's heart, once a steady drumbeat leading the herd through life's ups and downs, broke into pieces in that moment. Satao, her son, was full of potential, and their family's future was missing. His absence was a deep pain that echoed across the land, showing how much a mother can love and how unpredictable life can be.

Filled with a desperate need for answers, Grace walked toward Duke. It was a difficult moment, reflecting the storm of emotions inside her. She wanted to understand, to know the truth behind this brutal fight. Her voice shook with grief and a mother's fierce determination as she asked Duke, "What happened here, Duke?"

Duke confidently said, "I won. These young bulls are just showing off. They have a lot to learn before leading a herd." His words carried a strong sense of control, something always linked with him. He said he beat Satao easily, making Grace feel hurt, like a sharp piece of reality jabbing into her heart. One could feel Grace's disbelief, a mix of emotions inside her as she tried to match Duke's words with her cherished memories.

"Where is Satao?" questioned Grace.

"I last saw him near the riverbed; he must be getting his wounds treated by applying mud." Duke replied arrogantly.

Grace didn't believe his words. She was determined to find the truth. Driven by a mother's love and a desire for answers, she walked toward the riverbed.

Standing there alone in the wilderness, Grace's heart felt heavy with the weight of her mission. Each step she took had a clear purpose, going beyond her sadness. It spoke of a connection, not just to her son but also to the wild spirit of the land.

The riverbed was surrounded by a vast open field. Grace saw the massive silhouette of a majestic bull elephant from a distance. It was most likely Satao. However, he was motionless. As she arrived at the site, her worst fear came true—Satao was dead.

Satao lay still, his once-magnificent tusks missing—their absence a testament to a brutality that defied comprehension. His majestic form, which had stood as a testament to strength and life, was now a canvas of heartache that bore witness to the cruelties inflicted by those who sought to exploit the wild for their own gain.

There was a terrible hole in his forehead, showing a gap just like the one in Grace's heart. This hole represented the darkness that had ruined their lives. There were no visible wounds on Satao's body caused by Duke. However, Duke was in lousy shape and seemed close to collapsing.

Grace recognized the perpetrator responsible for Satao's wounded forehead and missing tusks. Only one species displayed the cowardice to deploy instruments of mass destruction for personal gains—Humans!

On the day of the battle, a few guides witnessed the epic battle between Duke and Satao and relayed it to all the other guides. Soon, tourists flocked to the site to see the spectacle, which became a lucrative opportunity for the guides. Due to his dominance, Satao quickly became a favorite among the spectators. However, among the tourists were trophy hunters, who coveted the alpha bull as their prize.

Driven by greed, one guide agreed to the hunters' request and planned to bring them back at dawn, hoping the fight would end. At dawn, the guide led the trophy hunters back to the site. The battle had just concluded, with Duke lying exhausted on the ground. As he got up and fled, Satao pursued him briefly before stopping to trumpet his victory.

Seizing the moment, the trophy hunters aimed their guns at the magnificent but tired Satao. A few shots later, Satao fell to the ground. The hunters took photos as mementos and removed his tusks as trophies.

The truth was clear and painful—an acknowledgment that destroyed the remaining hope, revealing the harsh reality of poaching. Grace's heart, already heavy from losing her son, now bore the weight of a grieving mother mixed with anger—a sorrow that was not just personal but also a symbol of the bigger fight to protect life in its majestic form. After this incident, the entire herd outcasted Duke.

In the aftermath of loss, the entire reserve itself seemed to mourn. The once-vibrant landscape was somber as if the very Earth shared the burden of Grace's grief. Around Satao's lifeless form, Grace found herself ensnared in a web of inconsolable sorrow—a mourning that transcended words and enveloped her in a veil of anguish.

Day turned into night, and night into the next day, as Grace remained steadfast by her son's side. Her presence was a silent tribute, a lament carried by the wind, echoing through the hearts of all who inhabited the wild expanse. The world around her continued to turn, oblivious to the grief that held her in its unrelenting grasp.

The entire herd was mourning alongside Grace. Even as her heart wept, Grace's role as the matriarch beckoned her to rise from the depths of her sorrow. The duties that had defined her existence—the protection of her herd, the guidance of her family, and the preservation of their legacy—called her forward, urging her to put aside her personal agony to pursue collective survival.

With sadness in her heart, Grace guided her herd away from where her son was lost. She left his remains for nature to handle. She had to carry on for her son Jerry, daughter Eleanor, and the rest of the herd.

Grace heard stories carried by the wind—of families torn apart, lives taken, and the echoes of existence silenced. Each tale mirrored her own, reflecting the sorrow weighing on her heart. In the eyes of others, she saw the same pain—the depths of loss resonating in her spirit.

Animals like Rhinos, Lions, Wildebeests, Zebras, and Leopards—integral to the rich fabric of life's diversity—have all fallen prey to the brutality of indiscriminate poaching. Once a harmonious symphony, the reserve wore numerous scars inflicted by human hands.

Who wielded the power to decide the fates of those who walked the land, soared through the skies, and prowled the jungles? Who determined which lives were worth saving and which were expendable, mere pawns in the grand chessboard of humanity's desires? These haunting questions weighed heavily on Grace's mind.

In her heart, Grace wishes for a world where every creature, from elephants to leopards, rhinos, and zebras, can thrive in their natural homes. The struggles of her herd and stories of other creatures strike her like a battle cry, a call to fight against the injustices of a world seemingly out of balance. Yet, as the guardian of her herd, she knows her responsibilities go beyond emotions.

Her reflections lead her to a decision out of pragmatism. She recognizes the advantage of human poachers with their powerful weapons. While her heart desires confrontation and accountability, her mind weighs the costs of such a battle.

And so, with a heavy heart and a measured resolve, Grace chose a path that avoided direct confrontation.

She decided to lead her herd away from the shadows that bore witness to human presence, avoiding the perilous intersections where life hung in the balance. This decision spoke to the wisdom she had accumulated over years of existence—a wisdom that acknowledged the odds stacked against them, the danger that lurked in the shadows.

Months passed, and they continued their journey through the wild. Grace's resolve found resonance among her fellow herd members. Their instinct, honed by generations of survival, recognized the prudence in avoiding the gaze of those who sought to exploit the untamed beauty of their home.

Chapter 6

Tragedy Strikes Again

Within the heart of the untamed wilderness, where each blade of grass whispered tales of ages past, an atmosphere of familiarity hung in the air—a familiarity that emanated from the presence of two white male guides and a tourist couple in their late 40s. These guides were very experienced and knew the reserve inside out.

Their presence used to be a comforting part of the wild, but today was different. Something unsettling unfolded, creating unease in the very essence of life. Grace's watchful eyes, trained by a lifetime of observation, noticed signs of change upon their arrival.

The guides knew the land well, just like Grace did. They shared a history of peaceful living, walking these paths with respect for the land and its creatures. In the past, humans and animals had an unspoken agreement to respect each other's space.

However, humans tend to honor this agreement only when it suits their convenience. The guides seemed different, showing subtle changes in their posture and expressions that made Grace uneasy. The air felt charged with a strange energy, hinting at events that could disrupt the delicate balance that once existed.

What struck Grace as particularly concerning was the presence of the tourist couple—a couple whose presence was notable not only for their small number but for the absence of the protective cocoon of their vehicles. They moved near the herd, traversing the landscape on foot—an act that deviated from the norm, a norm that had once been marked by a respectful distance.

As her keen eyes scanned the scene, Grace discerned something that sent a shiver down her spine—a chill that resonated through every sinew of her being. There, in the hands of the tourists, were instruments of violence. The presence of these weapons was a jarring intrusion, a threat that shattered the fragile equilibrium of the reserve. Grace realized this must be how Satao was killed as well.

In an instant, Grace made a choice driven by a mother's protectiveness, a leader's duty, and a sentinel's instincts. With the authority of her matriarch role, she urgently signaled the herd—a blend of vibrations, murmurs, and trumpets delivering a clear message: "Dangerous humans are near; we must quickly move to safer ground. These could be the same humans who are responsible for Satao's death."

The order caused panic among the herd, especially the young ones. It took them a while to regroup and follow Grace's lead. Her tusks, representing wisdom and experience, became alive as she guided, her massive form moving through the landscape like a living beacon of guidance.

The familiar terrain now felt unfamiliar, painted with uncertainty. Grace urged her family forward with each step, scanning the landscape for safety in the distance. Every herd member followed Grace's footsteps, or so she thought.

Jerry, the young bull elephant, and Grace's second calf, intentionally stepped into danger. He sought revenge for his older brother and the pain his mother endured from losing her firstborn. Grace was unaware of Jerry's bravery. She assumed Jerry was with the herd and asked everyone to follow them as fast as they could.

Jerry stood his ground and charged the guides and tourists—a brave move to challenge those entering the herd's territory. But they did not back down. A new situation emerged, disrupting the usual behavior Jerry knew. Jerry became confused and upset. He grumbled a warning to the guides and tourists to retreat from where they came.

After keeping a safe distance from the tourists, Grace tried to check on her herd. She could not find Jerry and asked the herd to stay in place while she went to bring Jerry back safely.

Grace alone raced back as fast as she could; the signs were ominous. Jerry was now within sight, and she spotted the guides and tourists ahead of him. One of the tourists had his gun aimed at Jerry. Before she could alter Jerry's fate, she heard a gunshot—a loud crack that silenced the surroundings. A bullet struck Jerry in the head, displaying a lack of compassion and respect for life. The impact of that gunshot spread through the wild, causing a disturbance in the existence of everything. Jerry, once full of life, now lay still—a clear example of the random cruelty that humans could use. Through their choices, the guides and tourists have changed this family's future forever.

From a distance, Grace saw everything happen—witnessing the sad event, watching the pointless loss that spoiled the land she loved. Her heart hurt with pain beyond words, a mix of a mother's sadness, a leader's frustration, and a watcher's acceptance.

She avoided getting close to Jerry because the guides and tourists were still nearby, capturing moments with their flashy cameras and mobile phones. She waited until the humans left. When she finally reached Jerry, the heartbreaking reality hit her – she had lost both her offspring to human cruelty. Ignoring her instructions to stay, the herd joined her to show solidarity and unity.

More guides arrived, who viciously hacked off Jerry's tusks to make it seem like the work of poachers. Grace watched in horror as this unfolded before her eyes. She felt powerless and couldn't bring herself to confront them. So, she waited patiently until the humans finally left.

Once they were gone, Grace approached Jerry. The sight of her son lying there lifeless broke her heart into a million pieces. It was a painful realization that both her sons had fallen victim to the cruelty of humans in the exact same manner. With a heavy heart, Grace made a mournful trumpet sound—a sad song that showed how deep her sorrow was. The herd, tied together by strong bonds, gathered around Jerry's lifeless body.

Her herd soon arrived at the scene. Despite her urging the herd to stay away, they came to stand by her side, showing their support and solidarity in the face of tragedy. Their presence showed the strength of those who stayed, the spirit that did not give up even when faced with tough times.

As Grace mourned the loss of her second son, she also felt a deep sense of determination to seek justice for them at the same time ensuring the safety of her herd. She knew that she couldn't let their deaths be in vain. She vowed to confront the humans responsible for this senseless act and protect her herd from further harm.

Chapter 7

Seeking Vengeance

In the sad aftermath of Jerry's death, the Mana Herd felt a heavy sadness—a sadness that could be felt throughout the reserve. When the guides and tourists left, an intense silence showed how much they had taken away from the world.

In this quiet time, Grace stood as a guardian of sorrow. Her significant form showed how deep her sadness was. She stayed close to Jerry's lifeless body, a constant watcher, a way of remembering the life that was gone. The herd gathered with her, making sad trumpets and rumbles that filled the air—a way of expressing their pain that spread through the wild.

But in the middle of Grace's sadness, a determination sparked—a determination fueled by anger, by a deep understanding that the cycle of violence had to end. She could not just watch anymore; she could not stay quiet in the face of human cruelty. Jerry's fate and Satao's sacrifice showed that something needed to change urgently.

With the heavy responsibility on her heart, Grace made a decision that would echo through generations and lead her into danger, uncertainty, and a fight for vengeance. She knew she had to act, use her anger to protect her herd, and make those who caused harm pay for their actions.

The role of leader, with a history spanning many generations, was passed to another capable female, Susan. Grace told them her plans, determination, and hopes for their safety. She asked them to stay in a safe place while she went on a dangerous journey—one that would take her into the heart of darkness, into the territory of those who hurt her family. She urged Susan to take care of Eleanor in her absence. "Stay safe and follow Susan's lead. Mommy must go for a while," said Grace to Eleanor.

Grace began her journey under the cover of night when the stars and the moon watched silently. Her steps were careful, her movements smooth—a reflection of the wild wisdom she gained from the land. Her senses, tuned to the night's rhythms, guided her, making sure she moved quietly, like a shadow, with the determination of an unstoppable force.

In the dark night, Grace became a symbol of payback. Her heart was angry and sad, and her tusks were sharp and dangerous. The importance of her mission felt heavy on her extensive body, making her move forward with strong determination. Her goal was simple—she wanted retribution for the lives taken and revenge for the pain her family went through. She tracked them all night using her smell and large ears. Along the way, all she could replay was Jerry's fall, his sorrowful trumpet, and the gunshot that ended his life.

Grace crept like a ghost, existing between what was real and what was not. Her instincts, learned through many generations of survival, guided every step she took. Each move was thought out, and every action had a purpose. She understood that catching others by surprise without making noise was crucial, as it might help conceal her presence.

And then, the camp appeared—a human outpost in the wild. It was a camp of the same guides and tourists who killed Jerry. Unaware of what was coming, the guides and tourists sought safety in their tents. The night kept its secrets, watching as a long-overdue reckoning unfolded.

Elephants have limited vision. She preferred to wait until dawn for improved visibility. After pinpointing their location, she maintained a safe distance and patiently waited to avoid startling the guides. Throughout the night, she had strategized her attack. At dawn, her first target would be the guides, followed by the tourists.

The guides can prove more dangerous if alerted. They knew how to handle animal confrontations, but their senses were dulled by the alcohol they had consumed to celebrate. While the tourists called it a night and went into their tents, the guides continued to enjoy themselves. They had left their rifles in the jeep, at least 10 meters away, and only had their revolvers, which posed no real threat to an elephant. Around 3 am, the guides decided to call it a night and went back to their own tent. Grace had memorized the locations of the guides' and tourists' tents very well.

They were unprepared for the storm approaching. The first light of day brought chaos for the guides and tourists. Suddenly, Grace emerged from the dense bushes. Swift and powerful, she moved with her tusks cutting through the air like sharp blades.

Grace first attacked the guides' tent without giving them time to react or call for help. She struck through the tent, hitting one of them hard. Grabbing him with her trunk, she pulled him under her heavy legs and stomped on him, rendering him immobile. She then used her tusks to stab him repeatedly.

The other guide was shaken and took a few seconds to recover. He tried to grab his gun but could not aim well. He shot at Grace six times, aiming for her head. Five bullets hit her, and none were fatal; one bullet grazed the top of her head, the other two bullets hit her big ear, and the remaining two hit her front leg. Thanks to her moving body, the guide could not take proper aim.

Grace grabbed the last guide with her trunk and crushed his skull with her tusks. All of this happened in just a few minutes. Once agents of violence, the guides were now the recipients of an unforgiving retribution.

Grace's assault was a symphony of vengeance—an orchestration of might fueled by the fire of her grief and anger. With force as raw as it was relentless, she eliminated both guides in a single calculated sweep; their lives were extinguished in a heartbeat.

Amidst the chaos of her retribution, the commotion stirred the tourist couple from their slumber. Unaware of the turmoil that had unfolded, a husband and wife found themselves thrust into a nightmare of their own making. Grace, her form towering like a titan, approached the tent with an aura of power that was both terrifying and awe-inspiring.

She effortlessly used her trunk to toss the tent aside, just like lifting a small branch. Now, the couple stood vulnerable to her anger. The husband told his wife to grab the gun from the jeep while he attempted to divert her attention. The wife hurried toward the jeep while the husband moved in the opposite direction, making loud sounds as if challenging Grace.

Grace's attention turned to the male tourist, the more experienced of the two and a contributor to the cruelty suffered by her younger son, Jerry. With the precision of a hunter, she advanced with determined purpose, her massive legs a formidable force of nature.

Charging elephants can easily outpace humans. Grace swiftly caught up to him, using her trunks to push him to the ground. She then seized him by the legs and forcefully slammed his body against a nearby tree, causing the male tourist to lose consciousness.

She crushed the male tourist beneath her massive legs in a decisive moment. His spine and then his head were crushed under the force of her powerful legs, akin to the ease of smashing a watermelon. His life snuffed out in an instant. Grace then went after the female tourist.

The female tourist, her breath a quiver of terror, watched as the scene unfolded before her eyes—a scene of retribution, of justice served. Her heart raced, and her thoughts were a jumble of fear and survival instinct.

The female tourist's path led her to the refuge of their vehicle—a sanctuary amid chaos. But her desperate escape was a mere illusion, a fleeting dream of safety. Her trembling hands reached for the keys inside the car, and she started the engine.

At that moment, Grace's towering figure emerged from the tall bushes, right in front of the jeep. The female tourist couldn't drive in reverse, as a tall, sturdy tree blocked the way. In a desperate attempt to scare Grace, she rammed the jeep into the massive elephant. But Grace remained unfazed. With her immense strength, she toppled the vehicle twice with ease. By sheer luck, the jeep landed back on its tires, but it was in no condition to move. The air seemed to crackle with tension, signaling an inevitable confrontation. Fueled by a surge of adrenaline and fear, the female tourist grabbed the gun left in the vehicle by the guides—a last-ditch effort to ward off the approaching force.

The first shot pierced the trunk with a force that would have scared a lesser creature. Though deep, the wound was not enough to deter her from her mission and her pursuit of justice. With the weight of the injury a testament to her resilience, she pressed forward, her purpose unwavering.

The female tourist, her heart pounding with fear, fired another shot, desperately hoping to survive. This time, the bullet hit Grace's head. Though not a fatal hit, it hurt Grace badly, and she started bleeding profusely. Grace kept going, undeterred and driven by a mother's anger and determination. She charged forward with all her strength, her massive body and tusks ready for revenge.

The vehicle, a symbol of the humans' dominance over the land, crumbled beneath the weight of Grace's fury. Her powerful attack showed that the vehicle wasn't invincible, reducing it to a wreck. The female tourist's body got severely crushed in the mangled jeep. At that moment, the female tourist met a painful and deserved end, reflecting the suffering caused to Grace's family.

Grace, from head to toe, was covered in her own blood and that of others. Losing blood was making her weak. She made her way to a nearby river. There, she drank a substantial amount of water, submerged her body, and covered herself with mud to cool off.

With the dust of the encounter settling, the land bore the marks of the clash—traces of a battle fought in the name of vengeance. The reserve bathed in the gentle light of a new day; Grace returned to the Mana Herd—a figure of quiet strength, a force of nature that had reclaimed the sanctity of her family's memory. The journey had been arduous, the price paid in blood and pain, but Grace had emerged as a guardian of the wild—a sentinel of justice, a beacon of retribution.

Chapter 8

Disoriented and Alone

The battleground witnessed the culmination of Grace's retribution—an act of vengeance that sent shockwaves through the reserve, altering the course of destinies, and leaving behind a trail of both justice and destruction.

But victory came at a price—a price measured not only in the injuries she bore but also in the gaping wounds within her heart. Grace, the matriarch who had led her herd with wisdom and Grace, now bore the weight of a mother's loss, a burden that transcended the physical realm and delved deep into the recesses of her soul.

Her triumphant return to the Mana Herd was a bittersweet moment, a reunion tinged with the shadows of the fallen. As the herd welcomed her with trumpets of recognition, Grace's eyes held a story that words could not convey—a tale of sacrifice, vengeance exacted, and a mother's grief that ran as deep as the rivers carved through their land.

The loss of her two sons—Satao and Jerry—weighed heavily on her heart, a pain that pulsed with every beat. With their intricate social bonds and profound emotions, the elephants knew grief in a way that few could comprehend.

In the days that followed her victorious retribution, Grace withdrew from the company of her herd, seeking solace in solitude. She even ignored her own young daughter, Eleanor. Amidst the rustling of leaves and the whispers of the wind, she contemplated the actual cost of the revenge she had sought. The hunters were gone, their presence eradicated from the realm, and justice had been served in the most visceral manner possible. Yet, Grace's heart remained heavy, weighed down by the shadows of the past.

The battle she had waged had taken its toll on her physical form and the fabric of her being. She bore two significant wounds on her head, one on her trunk, two in her ear, and two on her front leg. It was a somber reminder of the brutality she had faced, the retribution she had sought, and the losses that had driven her to this point. The scars she carried were not merely external; they were a testament to the depth of her grief, etched into her very essence.

The forest officials who had spotted her were taken aback by the sight. Female elephants were known for their strong social bonds and interconnectedness with the herd, providing safety, support, and companionship. The male elephants often embraced solitude, traversing the vast expanse of the wilderness in search of their own destinies. But here stood Grace—a matriarch, a mother, and a symbol of strength—alone and disoriented.

It was not long before this elephant's distress signal reached the forest officials. The wilderness held its breath as the forest officials, accompanied by skilled veterinarians, approached Grace's majestic figure. With cautious precision, the veterinarians readied their tranquilizer darts.

The forest officials understood the delicate nature of the task; their actions needed to be guided by expertise and reverence. Grace's safety was paramount, and the forest's guardians were committed to ensuring she would emerge from this ordeal more robust than before.

The tranquilizer darts flew through the air, hitting their target with a soft thud. Grace's movements slowed down as the calming medicine spread through her big body, and her eyes got heavy, signaling relief. She gently sat on the ground, breathing calmly as the land held her. The forest officials and veterinarians came closer, walking softly, with the explicit goal of treating her physical injuries.

With skilled hands and hearts full of respect, the veterinarians started their work. They carefully tended to the wounds on Grace's body, reminders of the battles and hardships she had faced. Six bullets that had harmed her were taken out with great care. This precise process followed both medical knowledge and a deep respect for the life they were helping.

The wounds were thoroughly cleaned and disinfected to prevent infection from spreading. Superficial wounds were stitched and bandaged, while more severe injuries, such as those on the forehead and front legs, required Surgery. Tents were built around Grace to carry out the Surgery. During the procedure, veterinarians removed multiple bullet fragments that could have caused internal damage and potentially proved fatal.

After the Surgery, Grace received pain relief medication to help manage her discomfort. After a couple of hours, as the effects of the sedatives wore off, Grace gathered herself and moved away from the humans. Feeling much better, she noticed these humans were unlike the guides she had encountered earlier. Grateful for their help, she acknowledged her thanks by raising her trunk.

As the forest officials and veterinarians worked, they were not just fixing physical injuries but conversing between the human world and the wild. Each action was like a bridge connecting two worlds—a bridge holding the hopes of protecting creatures that rely on the gifts of the land.

The passage of time saw Grace's recovery take root. The wounds that had once marred her forehead began to heal, leaving behind the traces of her battles as faint scars—a testament to her resilience. But while the physical wounds mended, the emotional wounds remained. Grace's heart still bore the weight of her losses—the absence of her sons, the echoes of their trumpets, and the pain that had driven her to seek retribution.

Even though Grace had emotional wounds, she found the strength to keep going. After getting care, she slowly got better. With help from the people who treated her, she became more purposeful in her movements. The wild, where she lived, seemed happy to have her back. The familiar sights and sounds comforted her as she recovered.

During her recovery, Grace remembered that her herd was waiting for her. Being the matriarch was not just a title; it was a big responsibility to her family, community, and all the relationships that made up her life. As she got physically more robust, her determination to get back with the herd, protect, and guide them again, which was like her legacy, grew too.

Chapter 9

The Unraveling of the Truth

The sun painted the horizon with hues of gold as Grace's reunion with her herd dawned. In the heart of the wilderness, a palpable sense of anticipation hung in the air—a testament to the bonds that connected the wild creatures and the triumphs that had been achieved through the interplay of resilience and unity.

As she approached her waiting herd members, the joyful trumpets of her family filled the air, creating a celebratory melody for her return. She welcomed Eleanor with love, embracing her gently. Grace was prepared to resume her duties as both a matriarch and a mother.

The young ones, sheltered from the weight of her trials, looked upon her with awe, understanding that the matriarch who led them symbolized strength and determination. The older elephants, who had weathered their storms, offered silent nods, acknowledging the shared journey that had forged their bonds. She quickly assumed leading them in their annual migratory journey, a tradition among elephants.

In that moment, the wilderness witnessed a celebration that transcended language and species. The wind carried the echoes of joyous trumpets, and the leaves whispered tales of resilience to the ages-old trees. The sun, which had witnessed the trials and tribulations of Grace's journey, cast its golden glow upon her—a benediction that marked her return to her rightful place among her kin.

As the days turned into weeks, Grace infused the herd with a renewed sense of unity and purpose. She led them to lush waterholes and verdant pastures, each movement a dance of leadership and guidance.

While Grace embarked on her journey of recovery and healing, the relentless efforts of the forest rangers pressed on, their pursuit of justice unyielding. They combed through the remnants of the base camp, meticulously cataloging every piece of evidence that bore witness to the brutal massacre. Evidence collected from the tourists' mobile phones, revealing the various hunts they conducted across the reserve, was a clear condemnation of the destructive capabilities of humans. The bullet casing, the footprint in the dirt, and each discarded item told a story. The last piece of the puzzle, the matching of the bullet casing and the bullets recovered from Grace's Surgery, was a clear indication that Grace was involved in the killing of the guides and the tourists. However, the reason for this incident was no longer a mystery.

Through the tourists' mobile, it was evident that they were the same perpetrators behind Satao's death. As the truth began to emerge, it sent shockwaves through the region. The echoes of the tragedy that had befallen Grace's family reverberated far and wide, each resonance a call to confront the harsh realities of a world where the balance between humans and nature was often tipped by human ambition and ignorance. The once indifferent or blissfully unaware community was now confronted with the stark truth that demanded accountability and action.

The story of Grace's vengeance and the revelation of the motivations behind the killing left a lingering bitterness in the mouths of those who had once been complacent or supportive of trophy hunting. The story spread like wildfire, carried by the winds of social media, the platforms of advocacy groups, and the narratives of those who recognized the urgent need for change.

The unraveling of the truth brought to light the heinous act and the more significant issue at hand—the contentious practice of trophy hunting. Questions were raised, discussions ignited, and debates raged on the ethical and moral grounds of taking the lives of majestic creatures for sport and pride.

As the forest rangers presented their findings, the weight of the evidence became undeniable. The legal system was set in motion, determined to ensure that justice would be served for similar animal lives taken. Many guides and trophy hunters were identified and now faced the consequences of their actions.

However, beyond the pursuit of legal retribution, the story of Grace's journey and her retribution left an indelible impact on the hearts and minds of many. It became a rallying cry for those who sought to challenge the status quo, change perceptions, and redefine humanity's relationship with the natural world. Her resilience in tragedy symbolized individuals' and communities' power to enact change.

Conservationists, activists, and individuals from all walks of life found inspiration in her story of courage and determination. In the wake of the revelations, the forest rangers redoubled their efforts to protect the wildlife under their watch. They patrolled the wilderness with renewed vigor, determined to prevent further tragedies. Their commitment to safeguarding the creatures of the wild, like Grace and her family, became a beacon of hope in a world where the future of so many species hung in the balance.

The tragedy that had struck Grace's family had exposed the dark underbelly of humanity's relationship with nature. But it had also ignited a fire that burned in the hearts of those who refused to accept a world where such acts of cruelty could continue unchecked. The narrative shifted from despair to determination, from grief to action.

Chapter 10

The Call for Change

As the echoes of Grace's journey reverberated across the reserve and beyond, her story quickly transformed into a legend that captured the hearts and minds of people from all corners of the world. The awe-inspiring tale of her bravery and unyielding determination earned her a title that resonated with the essence of her being—she became known as "The Queen."

It was a story that transcended species, a testament to the shared experiences of love, loss, and the unwavering desire for retribution. With each retelling, Grace's legacy grew more robust, her image imprinted in the collective consciousness as a symbol of courage and the fight against insurmountable odds.

In a world inundated with stories of tragedy and despair, The Queen's tale stood as a beacon of hope—a shining example of how a single individual, fueled by love and determination, could defy the darkness, and emerge as a force for change. People from all walks of life found solace and inspiration in her journey, recognizing in her the potential for transformation within each of them.

Tourists and Adventurers from around the globe were drawn to the region, eager to glimpse this extraordinary and courageous elephant that had defied the odds. The plains that had once witnessed her trials and triumphs now bore witness to a different kind of spectacle—the impact of her legacy on those who sought to learn from her story. Grace had become more than just a creature of the wild; she had become an emblem of strength and resilience, a living testament to the fight against the heartless acts of trophy hunting and illegal poaching.

The awareness she had raised became a driving force for change, inspiring the establishment of sanctuaries, wildlife corridors, and educational initiatives aimed at nurturing a harmonious coexistence between humans and the natural world. The title of "The Queen" was not just an honor bestowed upon Grace; it reflected her profound impact on the world around her. Her journey ignited a spark that kindled a fire of passion and dedication to protecting the vulnerable, defending the voiceless, and challenging the norm.

For the local community, The Queen's Tale catalyzed change. Grace's family's tragic losses were a stark reminder of the urgency of protecting their land, their wildlife, and their future. Conservation efforts gained momentum, with renewed commitments to safeguard the natural habitats that had once been taken for granted.

Were the motives behind trophy hunting genuinely aligned with conservation principles, or were they thinly veiled justifications for personal gratification? Does trophy hunting revenue actually go towards wildlife conservation efforts, or does it primarily benefit hunting companies and local elites? Could the decline of certain species due to trophy hunting have cascading effects on other species and the environment? Should there be stricter regulations on trophy hunting practices to ensure animal welfare? Could alternative forms of ecotourism generate revenue for conservation without harming animals? The Queen's legacy pushed society to grapple with these questions, questioning the ethics and intentions of practices previously accepted without scrutiny.

The Queen's story reached the ears of policymakers and leaders on the global stage. The narrative resonated with those who held the power to influence change, prompting discussions about the need for stricter regulations on trophy hunting and more robust measures against poaching. The passionate pleas of those who had been moved by her journey bolstered the efforts of conservation organizations, igniting a movement that demanded justice and preservation.

Grace's tale became a rallying cry for humanity's capacity to evolve, learn, and protect. The legacy of

The Queen was not just about her personal journey of revenge—it was a transformative force that shifted perspectives, redefined priorities, and sparked a movement toward a more harmonious coexistence between humans and the natural world. In her, people found a testament to the power of resilience, the pursuit of justice, and the ability to create change—even in the face of seemingly insurmountable challenges.

Beyond the Story

Facts and Figures

Estimates suggest that over 125,000 animals are killed each year for trophies worldwide. Between 2005 and 2014, reports indicate that more than 1.26 million wildlife trophies were imported into the U.S. alone, averaging approximately 126,000 animals killed and imported annually.

A 2018 report by the Convention on International Trade in Endangered Species of Wild Fauna and Flora (CITES) revealed that between 2008 and 2017, nearly 40,000 trophies from African elephants, just over 8,000 from leopards, and 14,000 from African lions were exported worldwide.

Trophy hunting often targets iconic and endangered species like lions, elephants, rhinos, bears, and wolves, raising concerns about its impact on their already threatened populations.

Trophy hunting contributes little to conservation efforts. While some argue it generates revenue for local communities, studies suggest these benefits are often minimal and unsustainable compared to the potential harm to wildlife populations.

Trophy hunting is a highly controversial practice that has sparked heated debates about ethics, conservation, and animal welfare. Many countries have implemented bans or restrictions on trophy hunting, particularly for endangered species. International organizations like CITES also regulate the trade in wildlife trophies.

Building a Compassionate Future

Do we learn from our mistakes, especially regarding the cruelties inflicted upon wildlife? Unfortunately, the evidence suggests that humans have a history of not just cruelty but escalating levels of it. Our inclination toward greed, a trait deeply ingrained in our species, has reached alarming proportions over time. Let's look at some of these transgressions.

Cruelties in Animal Agriculture

In the past, we hunted or domesticated animals out of necessity to fulfill our hunger and basic needs. However, as society has progressed, so has our insatiable greed. It is not merely about addressing hunger anymore but about catering to our taste buds. The demand for flavorful, meaty delicacies, even when not hungry, has given rise to mass Animal Agriculture. In factory farms, animals endure cruel conditions, living in crowded and unsanitary spaces that cause them pain and chronic illness.

Animals bred for slaughter are often denied the essential luxuries of life, such as staying with their mothers or enjoying their mother's milk. Some face untimely deaths for the sake of their tender meat, while others are culled simply because they happen to be deformed.

Cattle animals like chickens, pigs, and cows bear the brunt of inhumane practices. Confined in small cages or pens, these animals endure stress and discomfort. Dehorning or disbudding of cows, tail docking of piglets, and castration of male animals without anesthesia further exemplify the disregard for their well-being.

Birds like chickens may undergo debeaking, a painful process done again without anesthesia. In the egg industry, male chick breeds are often considered non-profitable and culled shortly after hatching. This is done through methods like maceration or gassing, leading to mass euthanasia of male chicks. These methods of slaughter can be a source of concern. Some slaughterhouses use techniques such as electrical stunning, which may sometimes not be practical, causing distress to the animals.

We need to enforce strict international laws banning inhumane practices in animal husbandry and provide substantial incentives for adopting humane and sustainable farming methods.

The Plight of Zoo and Circus Animals

Animals in circuses and zoos encounter numerous challenges, living in environments that are far removed from their natural habitats. These conditions often lead to behavioral issues and mental distress among the animals. Some zoos have gained notoriety for practices like live feeding, where herbivorous animals such as goats, cows, and donkeys are fed to large carnivores like tigers, lions, and leopards. While the intention behind this spectacle may be to simulate natural predation behaviors, it raises ethical concerns, particularly regarding the fairness of the situation. In the wild, every animal has a chance to defend itself and utilize its survival instincts against predators. However, in the controlled environment of a zoo, the fate of the herbivores is predetermined, lacking any opportunity for defense.

This begs the question: Do we truly need zoos? Could we not replace them with sanctuaries where animals can live harmoniously with nature as intended? Sanctuaries offer a more ethical approach, ensuring that animals are well cared for and protected from harm, with measures in place to prevent any overlap between humans and animals.

The Ethics of Hunting and Sport

Hunting as a sport sometimes involves individuals who see themselves as superior beings, exercising a perceived God-like judgment over what they consider "inferior creatures." This mindset is ethically problematic and reflects a disconnect between humans and the ecosystems they inhabit. Instead of recognizing the interdependence and coexistence of various species, their attitude reinforces a hierarchical view of nature, where certain animals are deemed inferior or less valuable than others. Rampant deforestation for timber, agriculture, or development results in the loss of crucial habitats and biodiversity.

Hunting as a sport in the name of population control should be abolished. Instead, we can implement non-lethal wildlife management programs that use scientific methods to monitor and control animal populations. Techniques such as fertility control, relocation, and habitat modification can be effective alternatives. It is high time that Governments and conservation organizations enforce stricter regulations on hunting practices and deforestation, ensuring the protection and restoration of natural habitats.

Experimentation on Animals

While scientific advancements have undeniably improved human health and quality of life, they have often come at a significant ethical cost. One of the most contentious aspects of these advancements is the use of animals in experimentation. These animals, often kept in small, confined cages, become subjects for various experiments related to cosmetics, medicine, and other products. The reality of their lives in these conditions is harrowing, marked by pain, isolation, and eventually death.

Animals such as mice, rats, rabbits, monkeys, and cats are commonly used in laboratories worldwide. These animals are subjected to a range of experiments that can include testing the toxicity of chemicals, evaluating the safety and efficacy of new drugs, and studying disease mechanisms. The justification for such experimentation is often rooted in the potential benefits to human health and safety. However, the ethical implications of these practices are profound.

The procedures that these animals endure can be excruciatingly painful. For instance, toxicity testing often involves administering substances to animals in doses large enough to cause significant distress or death. Surgical procedures may be performed without adequate anesthesia, causing immense suffering. Animals in cosmetic testing may have chemicals dripped into their eyes or applied to their shaved skin to check for irritation or allergic reactions.

Moreover, these animals often live in isolation, deprived of social interaction and natural behaviors. This isolation can lead to severe psychological distress, manifesting as repetitive behaviors, self-mutilation, or extreme lethargy. The mental and physical suffering endured by these animals raises serious ethical questions about the morality of using sentient beings for such purposes.

Ultimately, the fate of these animals is grim. Many are euthanized after the experiments are concluded, as they are deemed no longer useful for further testing. This cycle of life and death within the confines of a laboratory is often hidden from public view, leading to a lack of awareness and outcry over the conditions these animals endure.

The use of animals in scientific research has long been a subject of ethical debate. Critics argue that the suffering inflicted on these animals cannot be justified, even if the research leads to significant human benefits. We need to develop and adopt alternative methods, such as in vitro testing and the use of human tissue cultures, which can reduce or eliminate the need for animal subjects.

While animal experimentation has contributed to many medical and scientific breakthroughs, it has also involved significant cruelty and suffering. As we continue to push the boundaries of knowledge and innovation, it is crucial to also advance our ethical standards, striving towards a future where scientific progress does not come at the cost of animal welfare.

Impacts on Marine Life

Marine life faces threats from excessive fishing, plastic pollution, climate change, and oil spills, endangering ecosystems and livelihoods. Excessive fishing activities, often driven by high demand for seafood, can lead to the depletion of fish populations and disrupt marine ecosystems. This threatens the livelihoods of coastal communities and impacts the overall health of the oceans.

Human-induced climate change impacts marine ecosystems through rising sea temperatures, ocean acidification, and changes in weather patterns. These changes can disrupt the natural habitats of aquatic species, leading to shifts in their distribution and abundance.

Improper disposal of plastic waste contributes to marine pollution. Large amounts of plastic debris end up in oceans, harming aquatic life through ingestion, entanglement, and releasing harmful chemicals.

Accidental oil spills from shipping and industrial activities can devastate marine ecosystems. Oil spills can coat marine animals, disrupt food chains, and damage coastal habitats.

Human activities such as shipping, sonar use, and underwater construction generate underwater noise, disturbing marine mammals like whales and dolphins. This disruption can interfere with their communication, navigation, and feeding behaviors.

Abandoned, lost, or discarded fishing gear, known as ghost gear, continues to trap and entangle marine life long after it is discarded. This threatens various species, including fish, sea turtles, and marine mammals.

The line between culinary curiosity and animal cruelty blurs when live or barely-cooked seafood is presented as a mark of freshness. Take the Japanese dish "Ikizukuri," meaning "prepared alive." This shocking practice involves slicing live fish, often tuna, mackerel, or bream, for immediate consumption as sashimi. Similarly disturbing is the Chinese Yin Yang fish, where a live fish is deep-fried while its head is kept cool with ice or a wet cloth. This gruesome display creates the illusion of life through residual nerve impulses, causing the body to twitch even after being cooked. The practice extends beyond fish; some culinary traditions involve tossing live crustaceans like prawns and lobsters directly into boiling oil or onto a hot grill.

The instances above represent just a few of the numerous cruelties that humans have adorned our world. To combat these threats facing marine life, it is crucial to implement ethical and sustainable fishing practices that prevent overfishing and protect fish populations and their ecosystems. Governments and industries should work together to reduce plastic waste through stricter regulations, improved waste management systems, and promoting reusable alternatives. Mitigating climate change by reducing greenhouse gas emissions and investing in renewable energy sources is essential to preserve marine habitats. Additionally, enhancing the response to oil spills and regulating underwater noise pollution from human activities will help safeguard marine mammals and other oceanic species from further harm.

Recognizing Sentience in Other Beings

For too long, animal emotions were dismissed as mere instinct. But a scientific revolution is underway. We're now discovering that sentience, the ability to experience a rich tapestry of emotions, including pleasure, pain, joy, fear, and anger, isn't just unique to humans. Research reveals a hidden world of grief, joy, and even empathy in creatures other than humans. This newfound understanding challenges the very foundation of how we treat animals in agriculture, research, and entertainment.

Gone are the days of simply guessing how animals feel. Scientists now wield an arsenal of tools – from deciphering body language to peering into brains – to understand their emotional lives. We're discovering that many species possess brain structures that process emotions like joy, fear, and pain. This isn't just fascinating science; it's a game-changer.

This newfound understanding challenges practices that inflict suffering. Animals, just like us, crave positive experiences. They yearn for freedom, the thrill of play, and the comfort of companionship. Recognizing these desires should compel us to re-evaluate how we treat animals in our society. To put things into perspective, studies have shown that

Rats have shown empathy-driven behavior by freeing their trapped companions even when given the choice to receive a chocolate treat instead. Elephants have been observed engaging in behaviors that indicate mourning, such as standing vigil over dead companions and showing signs of distress. Crows have demonstrated advanced problem-solving skills, such as using tools to obtain food. Dogs have been shown to experience jealousy and other complex emotions, reacting negatively when their owners show affection to a stuffed dog. Octopuses have been observed to possess strong learning and memory capabilities, such as solving puzzles and remembering solutions.

The future of animal sentience research isn't just promising; it's revolutionary. A surge of enthusiasm and dedication is propelling us towards a deeper understanding of the animal mind. This knowledge compels us to confront the brutal realities of the wildlife trade and entertainment industries. The time for change is now, and the science is on our side.

Beyond Likes and Shares: A Call to Action

For too long, we've treated animals as objects, their emotions dismissed as mere quirks. But the science is clear: countless species experience a rich emotional tapestry. Isn't it time we stopped turning a blind eye to their suffering?

Our social media outrage is a good start, but "likes" and shares won't change the cages, slaughterhouses, and labs where animals endure misery. We need action. We need to become the generation that ends this cycle of exploitation.

The power lies within each of us! We can choose to adopt ethical practices, demand stricter animal welfare regulations, and be mindful consumers, rejecting products that come at the cost of another being's suffering.

A Brighter Future for All

This isn't about extremism; it's about empathy. It's about recognizing the spark of sentience in another creature's eyes. It's about ensuring every living being, from the majestic elephant to the curious crow, has the chance to experience the joy of freedom, the comfort of companionship, and the right to live a life free from unnecessary pain.

Let's stop asking, "When did we become so cruel?" and start asking, "How can we be better?" Together, we can build a future where compassion isn't just a hashtag but the foundation of our relationship with the animal kingdom—a future where all living beings can thrive, not just survive.